CASTLE OF A
THOUSAND
MOONS

SLEEPING WITH CROWS

LEROY HEWITT JR.

authorHOUSE®

CASTLE OF A THOUSAND MOONS
SLEEPING WITH CROWS

Copyright © 2018 LEROY HEWITT JR.

Published by AuthorHouse 03/07/2018

ISBN: 978-1-5462-2921-6 (sc)
ISBN: 978-1-5462-2920-9 (e)

Print information available on the last page.

This book is printed on acid-free paper.

AuthorHouse™
1663 Liberty Drive
Bloomington, IN 47403
www.authorhouse.com
Phone: 1 (800) 839-8640

CONTENTS

ACKNOWLEDGEMENT

Giving thanks to the Lord and Savior, for all his love and peace, for his mercy and wonderful blessings.

Thanks be to my wonderful parents for their love and support. Whom will forever be a very important part of my life, deep within my heart.

Thanks be to each and everyone of my siblings for all the fun, love and laughter we share, and for the kindness we have shown toward one another throughout the years.

Also thanks and love to the rest of my family members, and friends for their love and support. And to all of you who find time to read this book, or any part of it.

Thanks be to the publisher and its staff for the wonderful work they have done.

INTRODUCTION

"Castle of a Thousand Moons," is the tenth book written by LEROY HEWITT, JR. And it is just as exciting, and delightful to read as all other unique books written by him.

Other books written by the writer are as follows. Adrift in Scarlet Winds, Tears of the Midnight Sun, Mystic Eyes of Twilight, Jewels of the Red Dawn,

Captured in Mystery, True Persuasion, Red Hot Blue Nights, Mad Guns Till Romance, and Crime Love & Black Pearls.

This magnificent book, "Castle of a Thousand Moons," as well as the writer's previous books. Are filled with rare and captivating short stories, created in poetic format.

Combined with spectacular story poems, applied to rhythm and rhyme that can stimulate your imagination and set your mind aglow.

Prone to inspire the mind, as well as other books by LEROY HEWITT, JR. Taking you on the fantasy of an adventure,

giving you a glimpse into the window of mystery and intrigue. Expressed through true life experiences. Played out through factual and fictional narrative.

That can touch your heart and soul as the stories unfold. Capture the beauty of your imagination, and enhance the wonders of your thoughts, exhilarating your sensitivity moments at a time.

Raising the pleasure of reading to a whole new dimension. Where you can possibly be enchanted by all the imaginary sight and sounds.

Where characters may seem as if they comes alive, reach out and touch you by no surprise.

Putting you right in the center of attention, where you can feel uplifted and revitalized as you read.

So if you prefer that reading be fun, this book is for you. It is the book that takes your imagination on a journey to the,

"Castle of a Thousand
Moons"

THE WHISPER OF DAWN

Hear "The Whisper of Dawn," and behold the dark shades of stillness, that springs out of the mystery of darkness before the rising of the morning sun.

With shades of blue magic delight, which rapidly moves through the atmosphere with a bit of warm cheer, before the morning light begins to appear.

When out of the night it flows with softness, drifting from the sleeping shadows as it gently slides and glides, before your wandering eyes, prior to the early morning sunrise.

As if the shades of dawn begins to whisper secrets, taken from the shooting stars that brings wisdom to the wise.

Secrets that the shades of dawn takes from the twilight, when playing upon the dark edges of night, before the morning turns bright.

As dawn rises and falls, whispering secrets before the coming of the awakening sun, when the day's journey has just begun.

Lend an ear, if you think these words are real.
Then perhaps you, and only you, may hear "The Whisper of Dawn," as it will soon return.

Casting its shadows with the quietness of a baby lam, creating an atmosphere that exudes beauty and the silence of sound.

Come if you may, and feast your eyes on the shades of dawn, that spreads its shadows before the rising of the morning sun as it makes way.

When springing forth and spreading its wings between the ends of night, and the early morning's light.

As the gleaming sun finds its way through the aisles of a day. Soon after dawn has came whispering in with a smooth display.

Falling from the darkness of night, before the day is sparkling bright. To rock the cradle of sunrise for a burst of sunny delight.

Listen, and hear "The Whisper of Dawn." Whereby you may be surprise to hear the secrets that has been foretold, secrets that are more precious than gold.

When the shades of dawn begins to unfold, before the face of the sun is exposes.

Magnifying the horizon with a burning flame that glows, and blossom as a rose.

Then softly, the shades of dawn begins to drift away, fading beyond the early parts of day.

Moments after it has entered the atmosphere quietly and still, as gentle as a breeze when flowing with ease.

And with a touch of blue magic delight that you can sometime feel, when the sun is pervasive throughout the atmosphere.

Hear "The Whisper of Dawn," if you will. As it makes its way without delay, whispering in before the brighter part of day.

To bring forth the sunshine when the night has declined, as it spins and whirls within, the tail ends of night, and the front part of daylight.

Then hangs around for a little while each and everyday, before the morning sun begins to shine every which away. Set in pattern with a lovely inlay.

It comes in the early morning hour before the rising of the sun, when the night is done.

Then at certain times of the year, before the sighting of the morning sun.

It brings a quiet rain shower, before the light of day appears. Take wings and fly,

whispering through aisles of the atmosphere, when fading beyond the distant sky.

"The Whisper of Dawn"

Sing Me A Love Song

"Sing Me A Love Song," with a touch of soul, that can thrill me through and through, till the extent of my day has unfolded.

Whereby the sound of your soft voice can fill my days and nights with such delight, and with moments of pure joy.

Something I cannot avoid, when listening to your love songs as the music plays on. Inspiring me with a desire to hold you tight.

A song with gentle words, that expresses your love for me, with soothing lyrics in which I've never heard.

You as a jewel to behold, with sweet words to be treasured, that sparkles, and shines as if with pure gold.

Which makes me realize, that your love, for me is as rare as a diamond in the sky, so hard to find, and can stand the test of time.

Such an assuring love song, that lets me know that you are really mine, where there is no denying

That brings back delightful memories which warms my heart, of the things we so often do, whenever I'm with you.

"Sing Me A Love Song," as colorful as the rainbow, and as beautiful as the stars.

Reminiscing of the wonderful times we have had, recalling some of the joyful thoughts that lingers in the past.

And of the sweet moments that are yet to come. waiting beyond the horizon, perhaps within an oasis, that is filled with a world of fun.

That I may feel the passion that your love song exudes. Reassuring me of a love I shall never lose, a love that runs deep, calm and smooth.

Sing it with the melody of a slow Jam, that is mesmerizing, and awfully nice, tantalizing with a touch of sugary spice.

Then dance with me, and whisper in my ear, with the softness of your voice. Persuading me to believe in you, with such a sweet sound.

Till sweet romance will abound, whenever we are dancing alone, cheek to cheek till the night is gone.

"Sing Me A Love Song," with a heart so true, conveying your love for me, and just how must I love you.

To ease my broken heart, if ever we are apart. That paints a colorful portrait of our love, embellished by sweet kisses and hugs.

With a mellow tone that improvise, dispersing clever phrases that have kept our love alive.

Creating warm memories that will forever last, of precious moments that shall never pass.

A love song conveying that I'm the one in which you belong, that can soothe my soul, when my days and nights without you, are cold.

"Sing Me A Love Song"

SAY IT ISN'T SO

Dreaming eyes, aspiring to be wise. Caught up in an awkward situation of a bad provocation.

Taken for a ride, by the slick and sly. Tricked into a raw deal, how does it make you fell?

"Say It Isn't So," since this is not the way things are suppose to go. It is easy to understand,

how someone could fall for such a bogus plan. When their manner of behavior is trustworthy.

Figuring they will never have to worry, of schemes and scams, getting them into a jam.

When enticed with words coated with colorful sounds, of false promises designed to jerk you around, take your money and bring you down.

Words to deceive, pressing you to believe. Can give you a nose bleed, by the scams and schemes setup to be achieved.

Disguised and revised with a gentle offer, to lead you astray, with bad intensions to make you pay, as you wander along the way.

Raw deal, waiting to be cooked up just for you, how does it make you feel. "Say It Isn't So," how could you ever know?

Whether a transaction is on the up-and-up, or whether it was made to bring you bad luck, when conceived on the down low.

Where in the reality of ones mind, you are led to believe that everything is on a straight line,

that you are getting a fair price, by the one you think is precise, but that doesn't make it real.

When this is the way wolves in sheep clothing appear, getting within the cortex of your mind, where they can roam, that your wishes decline.

Especially when you are living on your own. So hard to think twice, when being bombarded with such bad advice.

By those who are incline to wheel and deal, take you on a fantasy ride, with twist and spins, thrusting you into a whirlwind, by no surprise.

When everything seems to be dandy and fine, true to your eyes. Tricked into thinking that there is no reason to worry.

Nothing to suggest that you were wasting your time, no warning signs. Taken in by the games people play, and the misleading things they will often say.

Designed to rob you blind, blow your mind, on the notion that they can easily get away, after you have been put in a bind to pay.

Giving rise to the schemes and scams, that have always been around, lurking since the beginning of time started to unwind.

Putting you in a trance, by being low down. With honesty denounced, false impressions teaching you a lesson.

A raw deal, that is not clear cut, tends to leave a bitter taste within the hollow of your mouth, after it has been cooked up.

Hitting you hard, deep down within the pit of your gut, perhaps the matter of a last result.

By those who wheel and deal, looking to rip you off, leave you with nothing at all, when thrilled by the scams they conceal.

To rob you of your hard earned funds, when the low down dirty deal is done. After the process has ran its course.

Showing no fear, when the guidelines against their ill will, are unlikely to be enforced. By means of a responsible source.

Putting you in a fix, by the facts they failed to reveal, that the bargain was unreal. When operating on the down low. "Say It Isn't So."

What say you? Tell me what is on your mind. When the facts are concealed, realizing that you've been wasting your time.

When you don't know the makeup, or the true terms of what your eyes perceive as being real.

When what you see, may not be exactly what you get, and what you are given may not be a perfect fit.

Sold as is, whenever betrayal is up for sale.
On the surface everything may seem to be panning out just fine, perhaps for awhile.

But at the ends of day, you may be in for a big surprise. When you began to miss your water when your well runs dry.

Perhaps thinking that you are unlucky, when in the back of your mind. Suspicions begins to lurk, got you feeling as though you are a jerk, when it will began to hurt.

Be on guard, right from the start, and on the lookout, for whatever raises a doubt. As this is the way life will sometimes go.

When suddenly, a transaction may turnout to be a raw deal, when the truth of the matter is not revealed, but has been concealed.

"Say It Isn't So"

On Silver Wings

It was a peculiar period of the year, as if time would stand still. When a lady contended that soaring "On Silver Wings,"

with uniqueness of skill, amid the atmosphere, was one of her wildest dreams. Something she would strive to redeem.

Whereas she would join the military to fulfill a burning desire that fostered within her mind, since she was a little girl, and at recent times.

Dreaming of becoming a fighter pilot, join the air force and give it a whirl, when living in a great big world.

Thereby she had climbed into the cockpit of a fighter plane, by which she would train. Completing the military's training course.

Inside an aircraft that was equipped with silver wings, when she would get behind the controls of the jet plane.

Wherefore she would fly across the open sky, while wrapping up thousands of fly miles.

However she would soon be discharged from the air force for reasons unknown,

whether or not the dismissal was right or wrong, since the morals of it was never shown.
Whereas the woman had been thoroughly trained, when no one would ever complain. A dedicated trainee, of a pilot she strived to be.

A person who had impeccable flying skills, whereby she had been presented with a trophy of silver wings.

Given to her by a flying club that she belonged, when joining up with the club soon after being booted out of the air force, without a recourse.

Her name was Ashley Morlane, who was also referred to as the silver wing queen, at various times when there was no denying.

During this particular time she had decided to settle down, find a nice man that she may get married. Start a new life and be a devoted wife.

Then as days went by, Ashley would go on the prowl. In search of the right fellow to be her beloved husband.

Visiting friends, church gatherings, and social events that would take place at various sites, including the holiday ends.

Nevertheless she had no luck in finding the kind of guy, by which she was hoping to hookup with, that a courtship begin.

No one to fit into her wedding plans, that they may be married, and give love a chance.

Soon an unfamiliar man showed up, said he came to rescue the woman from her setback.

Stating that he had gotten wind of a woman named Ashley, who wanted to be married.

She who had been out on the prowl, looking for someone that they may settle down.

As the man contended that he had shown up as a matter of fact, to assist her in taking steps to turn her life around, that she get on track

Whereby he had learned that she was on the lookout for a loving husband. In search of the right man to be her guy.

That they may be married, and perhaps have a beautiful child, as time would go drifting by.

The man who had picked up on the woman's burning desire, was named Frank Gaylow. Who had found his way near and around town.

When taking it upon himself to assist the woman in finding the right man to be her husband, where love could be found.

However the reason for his concern as he came along, was unknown. As if he was caught up in some kind of spaced out zone.

Some folks would contend that he was only out to try, and get on the woman's good side.

Whereby this stranger of a man was better known as Lowbo, who had been arrested, for kidnapping and purse snatching.

Selling hot items and other illegal goods down on skid row, and for murder not so long ago.

Then in the process of time, he would soon solicit a man who was his partner in crime.

Advising the man to go and approach the woman who was named Ashley.

That his partner in crime may befriend her, in such a compelling way that perhaps it would convince her to take a liking to him.

That she may confide in him in a trust worthy way. Be at ease, that she may come out to play.

And when the meeting between the two of them had occurred, Ashley and the tall slim fellow would began hanging out together.

A decent looking fellow, who went by the name of Teddy J. Verger, better known as Teddy Boy. As they would soon become a couple.

Get engaged and sat a wedding date, after Teddy Boy had proposed, when his heart was ice cold.

And prior to the wedding taking place, the two of them would take out an insurance policy,

that would cover the both of them in the amount of two hundred thousand dollars.

A scheme that had been concocted by the criminal known as Frank Gaylow, who was mostly referred to as Lowbo.

Then as time dragged on, when on a nice and sunny day. The two love birds, Ashley and Teddy Boy, would go for a ride, as they would glide, and fly high, when they had rented a small silver wing jet plane. Whereby Ashley would once again,

for the first time since leaving the military. Climb inside a cockpit and began to fly.

"On Silver Wings," as she would maintain.
When in flight, soaring across the tall blue sky.

When in control of such a distinctive plane.
Flying high as they went for an invigorating ride.
Gliding and dipping from side-to-side.

Thereby Teddy Boy had adamantly convinced the woman to do so, whereas his intensions were of an evil deed, in a quest to deceive.

When in cahoots with the criminal known as Frank Gaylow, better known as Lowbo.

Whereby he, and Lowbo had cooked up a scheme to inject Ashley, with a nerves gas,

That would render her unconscious when she would be in control of the speeding jet plane.

Then during such time, Teddy Boy had an impulse to parachute out of the plane, in hopes that Ashley would die in a plane crash.

That Teddy Boy and Lowbo, may collect the two hundred thousand dollars of a life insurance policy that was payable to them.

And that no one may ever know, and realized that the accident was in disguise.

Whereas Ashley, The silver wing queen, had a scheme of her own. As she had became suspicious of Teddy Boy before long.

When she secretly cut the lines to Teddy Boy's parachute. Then when he was not staring at her with his deceitful eyes, when looking away.

She would suddenly club him over the head, with a pipe make of lead, and quickly shove him out of the plane, perhaps to settle a claim.

As he went tumbling and spinning around, all the way down toward the ground, when his parachute failed to open.

Thereby he went splashing into the depths of the ocean. Where he was never found, when presumed to be dead, some folks had said.

Whereas Ashley would receive the two hundred thousand dollars of a insurance claim, that was payable to her, as she went laughing all the way to the bank.

Then after such deadly event had taken place, when time had progressed. Frank Gaylow, who was also known as Lowbo, would soon approach Ashley.

Pretending not to know her, as if he had never laid eyes on her, but had a desire to get acquainted.

When the two of them would start dating, as Lowbo was playing Ashley for a fool. Setting her up to lose,

When he would takeout his own one-sided life insurance policy on her, as they would soon be married. A wish that Ashley carried.

When wedding bells would rang, and songbirds would sang. But to Lowbo the wedding did not mean a thing.

Soon the unusual couple would purchase a large two story house on the outskirts of town.

When Ashley would go out and purchase her own silver wing jet plane before long,

after receiving the huge insurance payment.
When at certain times before sundown.
She would jump into the small jet, and takeoff from her runway before sunset.

When soaring high beneath the evening sky, "On Silver Wings," is what she maintained. When taking flight in a jet plane.

Then as time had come and gone. Lowbo, the husband, would convince Ashley, his wife.
Who was also known as the silver wing queen.

To use her small jet plane for transporting hot items, along with other illegal goods, for he and his clientele as well.

Customers of men and women, that were his partners in crime, operating across state line. Some who had done prison time.

Ashley would agree since money was tight, and when she figured that she would be fast enough, and clever enough to stay out of sight.

That no one could compete with her when
flying a jet plane, taking flight into the distant heights, soaring "On Silver Wings."

However, after making a few illegal sky runs, within a week or so. She considered this illegal endeavor to be over and done.

Since during the time when she was in flight, departing from one of the cities, where a few of the clients were operating across state lines.

When a strange, and unfamiliar speeding plane was coming up from behind. Firing gun rounds at Ashley's silver wing plane, as if by design.

When trying to shoot her down, blasting at her in an attempt to knock her out of the sky, as the two planes were flying high.

However by using her unique flying skills, she was able to escape, and avoiding being killed.

Then after such dangerous encounter, Ashley was exasperated, and advised Lowbo that his little escapade was over and done, and that she refused to make any more risky run.

But her deceitful husband refused to go along, stating that the operations between he and his clientele, must go on, or there would be a cold day in hell.

But Ashley declined, when she would go back to flying her small jet plane just for fun.

Only for matters of her own concern. Making sky runs on various evening, before the going down of the setting sun.

Whereas during takeoffs, when ascending into the sky, she would have to pull the plane up, and over a nearby bridge when going air born.

When soaring through the evening sky, going for an enchanting ride as she would fly.

However, her scheming wedded husband, Lowbo, would solicit another one of his partners in crime.

Give him a semi automatic rifle, and offer him twenty-five thousand dollars to kill his wife.

A man who was a known convict, who went by the name of Jack Knife, someone who would do anything for a price.

That Lowbo may collect a large life insurance payoff. In the amount of two hundred and fifth thousand dollars.

Then an evening, when Lowbo had gone out of town, creating lies and alibis, when ill-advised.

Which were meant to demonstrate that he was not around when the crime had went down.

Wherefore the murder of his wife was scheduled to take place in just a few days. As the hired killer, known as Jack Knife,

would soon made his way out to the house where the couple lived. As Ashley was into her return trip home, where she was left all along.

When flying toward her runway. To touch down on the landing strip, flying on her own.

As the killer who was known as Jack Knife, had came to get the job done upon her return.

Take her life, when clinging to Lowbo's advice. During the going down of the evening sun. As she had been out soaring "On Silver Wings."

Then be that as it may, when Jack Knife, the hired killer, had laid eyes on the woman.

He fell hard for her, thought he was in love. Couldn't take his eyes off the woman named Ashley, as it occurred.

Whereas they would hangout, when romancing about. In which he refused to take Ashley's life, thinking that she was awfully nice.

Then on the following evening, Jack Knife would go out and wait near the tall bridge.

Where he was ordered to lay in wait, and shoot the plane down, when it passes over the bridge.

As Ashley would fly over the tall bridge during takeoff, when going air born. whenever she would take flight into the evening sky.

Whereas she would fly until the going down of the evening sun, till the day was done.

Whereby Jack Knife had decided to go out by the bridge and watch over her, that she be safe.

Then suddenly, Lowbo, the woman's scheming husband had returned, sometime before the going down of the setting sun.

Made his way out to the tall bridge, before Ashley would take flight "On Silver Wings."

As he would lay in wait for the plane to pass over the tall bridge, that stretched across the winding river.

That snaked along the edge of their property as he came. And when he arrived, there sat Jack Knife, watching over Ashley. Anticipating the passing of her plane.

As he sat with his back turned toward Lowbo. When it appeared that he was in deep thought, with eyes toward the sky.

Then in silence, Lowbo would sneak upon him, and fire twice. Pow! Pow! Blasting with a three fifty seven magnum hand gun, before the going down of the evening sun.

Shooting Jack Knife in back of the head, where he bled and there the convict lay dead.

Suddenly, Lowbo, would grab hold of the semi automatic rifle, in which he had given to Jack Knife a few days before.

That he may shoot the soaring plane down, which was being flown by Ashley, his wife.

Then as the plane began flying near the tall bridge, and begun to rise during takeoff, when veering to one side of the tall bridge.

Lowbo took aim, and fired. Pow! Pow! Pow!!!! Striking the plane beneath and behind as it went by, when shooting it several times.

As the plane continued to rise higher and higher, then suddenly it began to dip, and fall from the sky, right before Lowbo's eyes.

Leaving a trail of black smoke streaming from behind. As it went crashing down into the nearby winding river, as the water went splashing and dashing.

When soon the police and rescue team would drag the body of Ashley from the murky waters of the river.

Then as time went by, evidence would point to the husband as the shooter. When soon he would be arrested, trialed and found guilty of first degree murder.

When convicted of taking the life of his wife, and the life of the man known as Jack Knife.

Whereby he was sentence to die within the bowels of the electric chair perhaps twice, for the killing of a man, among other things.

And for the killing of his wife, as she brutally died, when flying about the evening sky.

"On Silver Wings"

WHO CAN STOP THE RAIN

When we first came together life was good, as we hoped it would, and thought that it should.

When spring love began to bloom within our hearts, and a love affair began to blossom, with flowers of sweet romance.

Inspiring us to never drift apart. When our days were filled with sunshine, that beamed with perfect light.

Radiating with a luster of tender affections that evolved between the two of us. When our affair was trending quite right.

As pure love began to sprout, and throb within the warmth of our hearts, on a starry night.

When springtime love, appeared to be falling from the skies above, with sheer joy and such delight, all sunny and bright.

Then the rains came, bringing stormy weather into our world, as we were determine to stay together.

When the beaming sunshine that warmed our hearts refused to shine. Sent our love affair tumbling into a whirl, confusing our minds evermore.

Due to the dark clouds that invaded our space, bursting with a downpour, washing away our colorful dreams, that had began to blossom.

And the wild flowers that glisten before our eyes, conveying what true love really means.

That shined with bright and brilliant colors, trending far and wide as I would surmise.

Giving purpose to the view of our wandering eyes, as the love we shared was still brand new.

When suddenly, lightning would strike. As our love affair took a turn. When you received word that I, was spending time with another.

Believing that you were not the only one. Claiming that I was in love with someone else, that our relationship must be over and done.

Then as other dark clouds began rolling into our world, during such moments in time.

I would be advised that you were seeing another, having big fun, that I should be concerned. But we were not the ones to blame,

for the overcasts, which were drifting in our direction when we had no protection.

Due to the miss guided words that had no true meaning, words of no credence that were being constantly said.

When the rains came, falling upon our heads, drowning the flames of pure joy that burned within our hearts.

Subjecting our love affair to a dramatic change, that it would never be the same.

Gather if you may, on a cold winter day. All of you within the sound of my voice. As our blue skies have turned hostile, lashing out with a downpour, that falls upon our affections, chasing our sunshine away.

"Who Can Stop the Rain?" That falls within our hearts, of two lovers whose relationship,

was woven together by fate, right from the very start. None too soon or none too late.

As myself, and you, the princess of my soul. Were caught up in stormy weather that was out of control.

A matter of design, to wash away the love we once knew, now being described as a breakup that was long overdue.

Taken from a false reality that was predisposed, by no fault of our own as we try to carryon.

Who can bring back the sunshine to brighten up our days? And impede the pounding raindrops from falling on our parade.

Striking with lightning as it came along with the dark clouds. Thundering with falsehood that should never been allowed.

Such a cruel, and deceitful kind of thing, that was meant to do us no good, as our true love has been misunderstood.

In a manner in which unkind words were said. Such a strain, for the two of us, merely insane,

Designed to break our hearts, and tear us apart, something we tried to avoid and not be annoyed.

As our love was once pure and true, that our lips could not explain, just a funny kind of love, that our hearts would retain.

"Who Can Stop the Rain?" From beating upon my windowpanes, when we are spending romantic moments together, as two birds of a feather.

When the downpour continues to disrupt the love affair, that trends between myself and you, my lady,

by the love we once knew. That is now creating only heartaches and pain, such a crying shame.

Therefore let us wish upon the brilliant colors of a rainbow, that we may once again go where lovers play.

On a lovely sunshine day, where we have sojourned many times before, whereby we can dance the night away.

That our true love may once again be the same, after the rain has gone, and returned from whence it came.

Without delay, and let it be now or never, if it will, and if it may. As our relationship is destine to survive, eager to thrive.

If only we can holdback the stormy weather, that our true love may still remain, and that it may still be the same.

"Who Can Stop The Rain"

PILLOW OF DREAMS

It was late in the afternoon, when the shades of evening were swaying its way across the layout of the city, down Louisiana's way.

As the carnival had began to arrive within the boundaries of Lake Providence.

Where it would establish a temporary setup space in the streets on the west side of town.

Just before the evening sun would go down. Where people would partake of exotic foods, games and rides.

As the spirit of the seasonal fair had arrived, gently floating on air. When the carnival had came to town,

and for a couple of weeks it would abide, as it began to make its rounds, to other places that were statewide.

During a time when a peddler who went by the name of Bob Cat Jones, had came along.

Some folks have said that Bob Cat was from another planet, selling items that were out of this world. Such as flickering light,

taken from the burning flame of a fallen star, that shined quite far. Claiming to have captured it, and put it inside a jar late one starry night.

Traces of moonbeams, in which he claimed to have clawed his way up to the top of the highest mountain.

When capturing the reflections of the beams in a large jug. Atop the mountain that reached high above, where he sealed the top of the jug.

Claimed to have scooped up bottles of stardust. When on a safari, chasing after shooting stars, to a place where they would land, splashing within the desert's sand.

One other item he professed to have conquered, was known as the "Pillow of Dreams." in which he claimed to have redeemed.

An item he contends to have discovered. When visiting a place during a time when the night was longer than any other,

longer than a day, as you could hear him say. Where it is said, that dreams in such part of the world disappears into the darkness.

When others splashes into the sea, but none of the dreams ever fades away. As it was a belief that the dreams would settle into soft sponges,

that grew from a tall plant resembling a tree.
Where the native people collected the sponges, and created pillows. In which they would call it the "Pillow of Dreams.

Professing that a pillow could perhaps contain, well over a thousand of unclaimed dreams.

As Bob Cat would sell these items, among other goods from the back of his maroon van, and out of the trailer that was hitched behind the large rugged van. When members of the traveling carnival,

would choose a spot within the streets of the city, or on the outskirts of town, where they would setup shop, and settle down.

Where the peddler, Bob Cat Jones, would setup his tent, and assemble his gallery stand. To sell his items in the coolness of the evening,

and during the first shades of darkness, right after nightfall. When all parts of his gallery had been installed.

When you could hear the wolves howling aloud, deep within the background, when making their mating calls. Down and around Lake Providence, with a familiar sound.

Where Bob Cat would sell the colorful dream pillows, which were made with pretty tassels hanging loosely from the edges of them.

Some being yellow, green or blue, but most of them were a bright red. Where unique designs would join together, and combine.

Softly where you could lay your head. Whereas the peddler would shout out, roundabout.

"Come one! Come all! I beseech you. To acquire for yourselves, one of these beautiful and lovely 'Pillow of Dreams!'"

Then after his gallery stand had been setup, and all the items to be sold had been put on display, before the ends of day.

He would continue to cry out in a loud voice as people would gather around. In the streets of

the city, or on the outskirts of town. During the coolness of the evening, just before sundown.

Then at other times he would cry out during the arrival of twilight, through the early phases of first night.

"Come one! Come all! I beseech you, to claim yourselves a 'Pillow of Dreams,' for your comfort, and for the making of a dream to come true!" The peddler would shout out.

"Come! And purchase one of these magnificent dream pillows. So soft and cuddly, but most of all, these wonderful pillows will give to you.

The kind of dreams that you have never dreamt before. Pulsating with colorful images like your mind has never imagined," the peddler proclaimed, as he would explain.

"You may at times, wish upon a shooting star, that may shine from near or far, to make your dreams come true.

Wherefore I advise you, to buy yourselves a 'Pillow of Dreams' today, that your long awaited dream may come true.

As it could, and as it may, materialize right before the present of your eyes. So let it be true and let it be wise," the peddler would advise.

"Hurry! Hurry! Hurry! Step right up and buy one of these dreams pillows while they last, as I beseech you to think fast.

Especially if you have been chasing one of your dreams for quite a longtime, your whole life through.

Whereas you will be amazed at what the magic of a dream pillow can do for you." the peddler would say, as people made way to listen up.

Suddenly a lady stepped forward from the crowd, Whose name was Myrece. "Did I hear you say that if I buy one of these pillows, in which you are selling.

That the pillow will make my dream somehow come true?" The lady would ask,

when standing with three children by her side. As they were waiting patiently, innocent and bright eyed.

"That is correct!" The peddler replied. "It may, I certainly must say!" He would insist as a crowd of people were standing close by.

When soon other would-be buyers stepped forward, when asking questions in relation to the item.

Such as, how many dreams were in a pillow? How long will it take for a dream to come true?

And what kinds of dreams was the peddler referring to. Some of the folks would ask.

Then suddenly, one man who stood about the crowd, whose name was Willow, would yelled out. "Those pillows can't do anything for you!

No way can a pillow make your dreams come true, whether red, green, or blue," The heckler would shout out.

"You are taking this thing a little too far, and I see you as only a snake oil salesmen,

that's what you are," the heckler would yell. As he waited around for only a short spell.

However the peddler would continue to entice the people to buy one of his items, especially a "Pillow of Dreams."

As he paid the heckling man no mind, said the man was wasting his time.

Then on that particular evening the peddler sold approximately seven colorful dream pillows to women and men alike.

One of the women who purchased a dream pillow from Bob Cat, the peddler.

Was a lady who had asked the peddler a question, who went by the name of Myrece.

As she was standing among the crowd, when she had brought her three children along.

As they were much to young to be left at home by themselves, existing on their own.

The mother, Myrece, was dating a man in which she had a desire to marry, that he may become a father to her three children. If things would turnout right.

Then during that particular night, when she had put the children to bed. She would than happily grab hold of her dream pillow.

Crawl into her bed, and upon the pillow she would lay her head, and remember what the peddler had said.

As she would fall into a deep sleep. When a dream began to play about her head, tantalizing her mind, within a short span of time.

As she dreamed that the man she was dating had proposed to her, and that they had gotten married.

Then within a weeks time, after she had conceived the dream. The man proposed to her,
and they were married.

As she became a June bride, in just a short while. When the man had became the father to her three children. As if magic was in the air, when they became a happy pair.

Then as this occurrence had taken place. Some folks would say, that this marriage would have taken place in any case. As if it was meant to be, as far as eyes could see.

Then as time moved on, there was another young lady who had purchased one of the dream pillows from the peddler.

Her name was Dellarese, and her dream was to be a famous movie star, be featured on huge movie screens, and on the cover of magazines.

Then after she would lay her head upon the dream pillow, at least one or twice during the darkness of night.

She would soon receive a phone call, whereas she had been given a role to play in an upcoming movie.

In which she had auditioned, as the dream she dreamt appeared to be coming true.

However before the making of the movie was up and running. One night the producer of the movie would take the lady out on a dinner date.

To celebrate the making of the upcoming movie. Then soon after the dinner was over, he wanted to spend sometime alone with Dellarese.

Nevertheless, she would advise the producer that she was not feeling very well, and to take her home.

Advising the producer of a depilating illness she had contracted. Then after she had gone home,
she would get in bed, and upon the dream pillow she would lay her head.

When she began to dream that her sickness had went into remission. Then as the woman would awaken, and open her eyes.

She began to feel so much alive. Whereby her sickness had disappeared, when she had been revitalized.

Extremely happy about the way she had began to feel. As if she was living in a world of a different kind of atmosphere.

When she would soon get a hold of the producer by telephone, and inform him of the good new. Then after the two of them had spent more time together,

as the producer had gotten to know Dellarese a little bit better. She would become a big time movie star, destine to go far.

Seen splashing across the silver screen, playing the role of a beauty queen, in romantic scenes.

By the magic of the "Pillow of Dreams" which she had purchased, it would certainly seem.

Then as time would tell, another "Pillow of Dreams" would sell. Sold to a young man, who went by the name of Azavier.

He had dreamt of having a certain kind of automobile. A top of the line vehicle. Even though the price range of the car,

was beyond his means, when compared to his income. Whereby it was a very expensive machine, second to none.

So when Azavier observed Bob Cat, the peddler, explaining how perhaps a "Pillow of Dreams" could make your dream come true.

The young man became interested in what the peddler was saying. Whereas he figured, that buying a colorful pillow as such, perhaps was only for females.

However it was for males as well, when he would hang around and wait until everyone else had gone. When the peddler was all alone.

As he would then approach the peddler, and purchase one of the dream pillows. Which had delightful tassels hanging from the edges of it,

with exquisite patterns of designs, in shades of various colors that appeared to shine.

Then one night as Azavier lay sleeping in his bed, with the pillow underneath his head.

He dreamt that he had purchased the fine automobile, that he wanted so very much.

Which he had been dreaming about for quite sometime, perhaps more then a year, when it often played upon his mind.

He would soon awaken early the next morning, when his dream appeared to be coming true.

As he made his way to the job where he had been working for quite a long time, for every little dime.

Whereas the job only provided low wages as it was understood, and according to him this range of pay was not very good.

Nevertheless, on this particular morning the boss had given Azavier a large pay raise.

Moved him to a new job position in a new place. When he was happy as can be, for all eyes to see.

Then soon after his workday was over an done, he would hurried down to the dealership, and purchased a new car.

Where he would get a good deal, for a top of the line new and expensive automobile.

When he would drive it straight home, and show it to his mother. As his long awaited dream had came true.

He figured it was all because of the dream pillow in which he had purchased.

From the mystery man who went by the name of Bob Cat Jones, who had traveled halfway around the world.

Even though he was not well known, but out of this world it appeared that he belong.

As the spirit of the seasonal fair would always hang around, floating on air,

as it would seem. Where it would settle down, whenever it came to town, making its rounds.

"Pillow of Dreams"

TIS THE SUMMERTIME BLUES

As the morning sun would slowly rise a few days ago, and began to glide across the summer skies before my eyes, reaching into the late afternoon.

I would soon began to miss the presence of you, and the fun things we would often do.

As the softness of springtime had faded away, and the summer season had began to blossom, along with the morning dew.

When my mind seemed to be weary, for a brief length of time during a particular period.

Wherefore my days were not working out as I assumed. Then I would tell myself,

"Tis the Summertime Blues," that plays within the winds of my mind, with thoughts of sweet sounds, and harmony that spins my head around.

Motivated by a defiant love that plagued the conviction of our courtship, tearing at our hearts, and ripping them depart.

When you, the love of my life had gone, left me all alone. Creating a sad song deep within the cradle of my imagination, Toiling at my soul with such aggravation.

Exposing my existence to the summertime blues. That fills my days and nights,

with a sad song of rhythm and rhyme, born out of the blues that you left behind.

Whereby you, my lady, refused to play the game of love by the golden rules, a path you would choose.

Took the sunshine out of the environment of my summer days, when you packed your bags, then away you strayed.

Left me afflicted by an emotion in which I struggles to overcome, trying to find a way to make it through, such a hard thing to do.

When daydreaming of the wonderful moments I shared with you. As we were spending happy times together,

thought it would last forever. When suddenly you left me standing alone, stole my love and now you're gone.

Left my heart singing the blues, for a love I stood to lose. As I realized by no surprise, when convincing myself!

"Tis the Summertime Blues," that grabbed a hold of me, intoxicating my mind.

As if I was a drunken fool, when it refuses to turn me loose, that I may unwind.

Moving through the lazy days of summer.
Thrusting me into such a debilitating mood.

Spreading thoughts of colorful words of a song we used to sang, that dances within my head.

With phrases that have lost their true expressions, and would fade away instead.

After you captured my heart, took flight, and would steal away into the night.

Whereas for me, the jubilation that once filled my days has disappeared. When there was no more sunshine in my life that I could find.

To brighten up my atmosphere, as the situation had me living in the blind, as it was revealed in a short manner of time.

When I would no longer feel an urge to go out on the town, during a starry night since you were not around.

Whereas my skies are no longer crystal clear, as I sat alone, spending my summer days without you, a predicament that seems unreal.

As I take strolls through the park when I'm out wandering about, gazing up into the trees as I find my way around.

Watching the blue birds as they sing their songs, among the fading leaves.

When I would walk alone, contending with the summertime blues, till the sun goes down.

As I could hear the sounds of it ringing in my ears, that clogged my atmosphere, subjecting me to a strange sense of clarity, as it would appear.

When the blue birds seemed to be whistling a familiar tune of a love we once had, a love that would not last.

As I was thrust into a downward mood. that spins my head around to a differing turn, of the love I stood to lose.

Thus I now realize the reason, for the rhythm and rhyme, that entered into the winds of my mind. Of a sad tune, on one summer afternoon.

"Tis the Summertime Blues"

Secrets In Your Eyes

Here you comes again, acting as though your love life is still the same, as perfect as it has ever been.

In the same old way, as you did the time before, which was the last time I gazed upon your face, since the passing of just a few days.

When you were pretending, that your love life was as a spring rose, a lovely sight, with wonder and delight to behold.

As gentle as a morning breeze, that blows with ease, when you were speaking tender words in which you chose.

Whereas it appeared that you were being vague, shifting around from place to place, gazing into the sky.

As your vigor would began to rise, and the spirit of you was raised quite high.

As if only happy thoughts were running through the traces of your mind.

When giving the impression that everything in your love life was quite fine.

Whereas rumors had begun to spread of a different view, into what was ailing you.
Contending that you were living in a fantasy world, most of the time. Pretending every aspect of your love life was grand.

Stating that you and a certain fellow, had came together when making wedding plans, which seemed to be a trend.

But when I moved in a little closer to you, and took a look into your eyes, in relation to the words in which you had advised.

I could visualize, the "Secrets In Your Eyes," when you would stroll in my direction, then walked on by.

As if the sight of your eyes, were whispering soft words that appeared to fall upon your ears only, when no one else could hear.

Advising you to holdback the tears, when it seemed that you had a hankering to cry, pretending to be shy.

Secrets you were trying to hide deep down inside, within the bosom of your thoughts,

that plays upon your emotions. Conveying that it was your broken heart, from whence love would depart.

And the loss of your devotion, that you are trying to keep on the down low, that the "Secrets In Your Eyes" will not show.

As the words spoken by your lips, did not have the ring of truth. Telling lies,

clinging to alibis, in an attempt to keep the truth of the matter concealed.

But the silent words in which your eyes reveals, are quite real. Reflecting the way in which you truly feel.

Suggesting that the words spoken by your lips are not precise, but a scheme to deceive, and mislead.

Due to pressing matters that you are trying to hide, of love denied, that has past you by.

When trying to convince yourself that it is still viable. Pulsating with passion that you thought would continue to thrive.

Whereas the "Secrets In your Eyes," tells of tales and players, casting dark shadows of betrayal.

Whereby the romantic endeavor that was between yourself, and the last guy,

in which you would reside, has crumbled and failed, when love was denied.

Magnifying with old memories that are hard to die. Giving you a desire to keep to yourself, share your secrets with no one else.

When you were subjected to promises that had been proposed, in such a way that makes your blood runs cold.

"Secrets In Your Eyes," as I have come to realize, to which I apologize.

For the matter that has been revealed to me, of a love that has gone wrong, creating heartbreaks that don't belong.

Due to forbidden love that you would give a try, which would not survive, perhaps coming somewhat of no surprise.

Of tales and players, ill responsible guys, whose love could not prevail. When love is not for sale, something you cannot buy.

As you would go shedding tears, to wash away the stigma that looms within your eyes, when you would start to cry.

Thinking of the love, that was once your heart desire. Exciting and romantic, that seemed to be so alive.

Love that has died, eliminating the colorful sparkles that once played within your smile. But on the contrary it would not survive.

As it used to fill your days and night with a bit of joy, that would blossom as spring flowers, within your heart and soul, till love ran cold.

Then with a twist of fate, it would refuse to hang around, and slip right on by. Vanishing into the distant sky,

along with the evening sun, as it would slowly fade away. Going down, whereas the love you lost, may never be found.

"Secrets In Your Eyes"

Sleeping With Crows

It was late one evening on a crisp autumn day, when the last of the evening sun could be seen drifting down behind the forest trees.

Before the first sign of darkness could be conceived.
When your eyes would behold a strange man, whose name turned out to be Tedwin Shurell.

As he was briskly walking toward a dilapidated barn, where men used to store bales of hay down on a nearby farm.

As the man appeared to be foraging ahead with urgency, moving toward the old run-down place.

That set back near the edge of the green water lake, which snakes along side the wooded area and crawls into a riverbed.

As the shade of evening were into its last phase, swiftly passing through the ends of day, as the man made his way.

Heading for the old shabby red barn, where he would stay, which was buried deep within the bowels of the back woods, where he would sleep with crows, simply because he could.

Whereby he was using the place for his hideout, that occupied the grounds just a few miles outside of town.

Then during the late evenings, or the early part of the nights,
At times he would be making his way back from the garbage cans, and trash bins where he had been scrounging for food.
During the time when the fading shades of twilight were about to rendezvous with first night, when the afternoons were hot, and the evenings were semi cool.

Till the ends of day would conclude, when the sunset would melt into the dusk, laced with a hint of summertime blues.

Where many a crow, would roost outside the old red barn, perched high above the rooftop. Flapping their wings as a number of them would come and go,

some moving fast, other moving slow. As the rhythm of the summertime blues was into an easy flow. As the crows were trying to stay alive, flying high as often as the winds blow.

When others roosted inside, perched in the hayloft, and on wooden planks that extended across the upper inside of the run-down building, high above the wooden floor.

Yet others would roost within the branches of the surrounding trees, lounging amongst the canopy of leaves.

Once upon a time not so long ago, Tedwin had been the CEO of a large cooperation where he earned enough income to purchase a two story mansion.

In which he had set his sight, including renter properties, claiming to own the real estate outright.

Fine automobiles he retained, claiming that all were his, as it would certainly appear throughout a couple of years.

With power to impress, bragging about his short lived success. Taking bribes, which blinds the eyes of the wise.

Little did he know, that his acquired illegal fortune would soon disappear within the sands of time.

When the seasons seemed to have intertwined, as the days of summer had slipped out of the atmosphere, when winter was about to appear, as it had began to unwind.

Whereas the man in which he used to work for, turned out to be a big time hood, whose name was Brouno Moclide, known to have put other men lives on the line.

A devil cloaked in a three piece suit, the man who had Tedwin jumping through quite a few hoops. Moclide was entrenched in money laundering, theft and racketeering.

Along with other men whom he would do business with, wheel and deal, men he thought he could depend.

Men who would steal, have other men killed. Do whatever they could in order to sustain their lifestyle, spending money to see other men die.

Whereby in this dirty racket, Tedwin was just another pawn in the game. Living his life for another man's gain, simple and plain.

However, when Tedwin would enter the old barn where the crows lived. There the large shiny blackbirds would start crowing aloud.

Crying out with disapproval in relation to the man being there, but he did not care. Kept right on intruding upon the crows, that his will be imposed.

When he had finished rummaging through the trash bins and garbage cans. Looking for food to eat, old clothes to wear, and shoes to put on his feet.

Nevertheless, the man named Tedwin Shurell would go there every evening or every night to make his bed, said he needed somewhere to lay his head.

When hiding out, round about. Keeping on the down low, that no one would ever know. At times wearing a disguise when he would step outside.

Had been recently run out of town, of the city in which he once lived. When Moclide, the big time hood no longer wanted him around, whether he live or whether he die.

Whereby through all his ups and downs, in which the big time hood had put him through.

He began to drink heavily, becoming an alcoholic, as if he had nothing else to do. Sent to a treatment center with plans to start his life anew.

With hopes of overcoming his drinking addiction in various ways. An alcoholic prevention program that he decided to pursue for a number of days.

When lines of deep frowns had showed upon his face, but what he did not know, was that old habits die slow.

Whereas he was now wearing old worn out shoes, and ragged clothes torn with holes. Living in a world of confusion, "Sleeping With Crows."

As his fortune had disappeared, left him way behind, standing still, gone with the sands of time.

Took a turn, went blowing in the wind after the passing of a few good years. Whereby he had became an alcoholic,
with no place to stay.

Living his life as if a predator of prey, when at nightfall he would find his way out to the old red barn. Staggering about trying to figure things out.

Tedwin had been let go from his job as CEO, a position he once held at a well known company. Where he would have his one shiny moment under the sun.

Whereas he had been accused of embezzlement, taking bribes and telling lies. Stealing parts of the employees salary when it came up missing.

Cheating them out of the funds, that had been put away for their pension, thought no one was paying attention.

When he decided to go on the run, thinking this was the way to get things done. As he would soon skip town, slip out of the city where criminal charges would abound.

Charges that were levied against him, along with other civil claims that had been filed, many as the law would allow, and there they would remain.

When he decided to flee the city, in an effort to escape his turbulent past. Refusing to hang around as he would make his way here, that he may not be found.

Hiding out and running about, in an attempt to evade the long arm of the law, living raw, one of the strangest fellows eyes had ever saw.

Then as he would made his way to the vacate red barn on this particular evening, during the time before the gathering darkness would meet up with the night.

The crows had settled down, and began to roost in the upper inside space of the old run-down place, near the ends of day.

Also they perched above the rooftop, nestling amongst the straws inside the barn, and atop bales of hay.

As the drunken man would abruptly burst through one of the closed doors. Staggering into the place, when fussing and cursing with madness on his face. As such behavior would go on for hours till the night was almost done, before the rising of the morning sun.

When all the blackbirds began crowing aloud, during a time when you could hear the wild beast as they began to howl.

When the crows began flapping their wings about, crying out, as they did not want the man there. Disturbing their domain acting quite strange, hard to explain.

As he was disrupting their roosting space, time-after-time, acting as though he had lost his mind. Carrying on with his wild antics, and sloppy drunkenness.

There the man began swinging his coat around, angrily throwing it at the crows. Kicking at straws,

and at bales of hay, that had been left behind when sprawled across the hardwood floor, inside the old red place.

"Shut up you mangy old crows, I'm running this show. A new boss has came to town, and I want you to know. As I'm telling you with no messing around.

Now shut up! So I can get some sleep tonight, till the morning light," the man would shout out drunkenly.

When he would fall across some of the scattered straws that lay amongst the bales of hay, and across some of the loose feathers left behind by the crows, till the break of day.

Where he would occupy a part of the hardwood floor, inside the dilapidated place. As time would race through the summer days when catching up with the fall of autumn.

Then in the meantime, as the days of autumn would linger into the coming of winter. Two FBI investigators would show up here, searching roundabout.

When they would make their way through the mean street of this city. Moving within and moving without, on the rough side of town.

Asking about a man named Tedwin Shurell. Wanted to know where he could be found, stating that he might have been hanging around within the dark shadows of the city streets.

Whereby he had slipped out of the city in which he once lived, fleeing the place from whence he came. Stating that they had received other information, which was basically the same.

Contending that the wanted man had been seen moving in, and moving out. Slipping into the night, avoiding the sunny side of daylight when rumbling about.

Whenever the sun was sinking low, as it appeared that he had no place to go. Attempting to keep out of sight, during the evening light,

till the sun would go down. When he would steal into the undercover of darkness as he raced with the night, when he would slip away into his hideout a few miles outside of town.

Nonetheless, no one would come forward with word that the fugitive had been seen hanging around. Reluctant to speak to the FBI investigators by any means.

However, there came forth a woman who was not afraid to speak to the investigators. She had heard news that the man in which the agents were in search of.

Had been seen running around in the rural part of the city. At times going back and forth, slipping in and out, swiftly moving about.

Said he may have been staying in an old run-down barn. Where he had been accused of beating upon the crows,

as if he was insane, the woman would go on to explain. With clear and precise details, sharing the information she had retained, that the FBI may be able to pickup on his trail.

Referring to the crows that occupied the old run-down red barn that stood outside of the city. Believing that this was the place where the fugitive could be found.

When advising the FBI agents of the man who had been hanging around out on Canopy Road. He who had been "Sleeping With Crows."

Then during the early part of the night, when the evening light had been devoured by the jaws of darkness. As time would move on before long.

The man had made his way back to the barn. Treading through the squishy mud and slimy waters, avoiding the wind and the rain, as he came.

Drunk as a skunk carrying a TV set. In which he had recently swiped, during the darkness of night. When he would cover it up, that it may not get wet from the falling rain.

But what he failed to realize was that no electricity was available inside the barn, as he could not turn the set on.

The place did not even have lights, remaining dark all through the night. No electrical components were in sight.

Then after he had finished yelling and cursing at the crows, the man would soon fall asleep as he made way.

Falling across the loose feathers of the crows, and across the straw that lay amongst the bales of hay. That were spread over the red barn's floor, scattered down below.

Then on the following day, when morning had rolled out from the night, bursting with early morning light.

It was plain to see, that the crows had defecated on the man, and upon the TV set with no regret, as the man lay asleep.

And when he had awaken, he became furious, fussing and cursing at the blackbirds, and throwing various objects in their direction, in an attempt to do them harm.

During a point in time when he had became so alarmed. When suddenly, some of the objects that were being hurled at the shiny blackbirds, would strike a few of the crows.

Injuring them as they went falling down below, landing on the red barn's floor. As others would swiftly fly away through an open door.

Soon the man would partially clean himself off, along with the stolen TV, when he would setout toward downtown.

In a quest to sell other hot items including the set when he would hang around. That he may have money enough to buy alcohol for himself, to get stone, before long.

Then there! As time moved on. The crows had became violent, as they setout to punish the thieving man,

for what he had done. When they would soon take to the sky, where they would hastily fly high with madness in their eyes.

Looking for he who had invaded there domain, he who appeared to be insane, when going into a drunken rage with madness upon his face.

When injuring some of the crows, as they had fallen to the hardwood floor inside the old run-down place.

Whereas the shiny blackbirds would soon enter the city, where the cold winds blow. As they were on the go.

Looking for the man who was disrupting their lives, scoping far and wide for him, by the sight of their keen eyes.

As they would boldly fly, gliding on high, where they would soon spot Tedwin, moving through the streets of downtown.

As the mad crows were making a disturbing kind of sound as they were searching all around. Flying above the places where they thought the man may be found, before the sun would go down.

Swerving overhead, riding on the wind, readying themselves to swoop down on the man and take revenge, hoping to bring this thing to an end.

When suddenly, the large blackbirds would swiftly go into a dive, swarming low and swarming high as they were getting into their attack mode.

When suddenly, they would swiftly swoop down on the man. Striking him about his head, and about his eyes, with their long sharp beaks,

and with the claws of their feet. Quickly he began running, trying to get away. "The crows! The crows! The crows!" You could hear him say.

As he continued to holler out, running about. When all the onlookers began running around, as they were also trying to get away.

Looking for another place to stray, when suddenly the man would go into a panic. During a point in time when he would spot two security cops standing right before his eyes.

As the black crows were rapidly swarming and lurking above him head. As he would call out for the two security cops who were standing nearby.

Whereas the crows had began viciously attacking the man, with blood in their eyes, ripping into his head, when he yelled and bled, as the crows continue to fly.

The security cops would then fire several shots into the air, in an effort to frighten the attacking birds away.

When the crows would swiftly fly into the distance of day without any delay. Then before long when they had gone, the cops would soon ascertain,

that the man who had been recently attacked by the mad crows. The one who had been seen running in the rain, was one in the same.

The exact person who had been recently accused of swiping the TV set, which had been reported stolen, and not rediscovered as of yet.

They would place the man under arrest. After he had been treated and released from the hospital, for injury to his head, eyes, and chest, as he would confess.

Then later, when the two FBI who were looking for this person. Had discovered that the man known as Tedwin Shurell,

was now locked up in the city's jail. They would serve the man with a warrant, to have him expedited back to the city from whence he came.

Where he would soon stand trial, for the crimes in which he was accused of committing. Sometime before packing up and fleeing their city.

Where he was found guilty of all charges that were levied against him. Sentenced to eleven years in the state pen, for charges he could not defend.

Charges relating to the money he had swiped, and did not hesitate to spend, money he had received for other hot items in which he sold.

Whereby the man's thieving ways had been curtailed, when the hearing was over and done, and the case was closed. In relation to the items he had stole.

As his fortune had disappeared within the sands of time. Left him behind standing still, when the winter was cold.

As his short lived productive years came to an end, took a turn, and went blowing in the wind.

"Sleeping With Crows."

AM I IN LOVE

It was a warm and mystic starlit night, touched
by the soft rates that fell from a crescent moon, that
shined with an array of purple blue light.

When it appeared to be dancing with the stars, which
were sparkling with fiery flames creating such a
beautiful site.

In which it appeared to be taking place right before
my eyes, with wonder and delight. As I stood gazing
into the sky.

When a lovely lady would wander into my world. Then
there, she would speak to me when uttering a few
words.

With the voice of an angel, thereby we had met for the
first time, as she appeared to be divine.

In which I began to have a tangling and passionate
feeling toward her. As with a flower that burst open
at springtime, with reason and rhyme.

A touch of wonder that I had never felt before as she
was standing near. Then after she had gone away,

she would stay on my mind most of the time. When an
image of her began to blossom within the walls of my
imagination, with a hint of warm sensation.
When I would get a burning desire to be with her, hold
her in my arms. A feeling I had never felt before, so
soft and warm.

Will somebody please tell me, if you will, and
If you may, "Am I in Love?" Beneath the dreamy stars
above.

By means of the reason I feel this way, or could it be
just a dream in which my mind portray.

Since the first moment I look into her pearly eyes, It
seemed as though I was hypnotized.

Fascinated whenever I would see her coming my way.
As I would try to make small talk that I may get close
to her, then I was lost for words to say.

And when she slowly turned her head around toward
me in a special kind of way, and gazed into my face.

I would be mesmerized, by the jewels which appeared
to be sparkling within the glow of her tender smile.

Whereby I have never been in love before, and do not
recognize the feeling, or telltale signs that will let me
know, or tell me so.

And when I'm close to her I feel such tantalizing vibes,
that flows between the two of us that drives me wild.

Exciting my heart, something I cannot avoid.
Conveying a message to me that suggest we shall never
be apart.

Then as a bit of time had gone by, she would kiss me,
and caress me with a warm embrace. When suddenly
my intensity had been raised.

Putting my mind in a daze when I was dazzled by her charm, as she allowed me to hold her in my arms. As I was overwhelmed and amazed.

Could it be that I'm the kind of guy who falls head-over-hills, for thrills of a kiss and a hug.

Then if so, allow me to pose a question to you, whether false or whether true, "Am I in Love?" Beneath the shooting stars above,

Be that as it may, she gives me a whirl, as if making magic appear, that burst forth with an array of wonder that lights up my whole world.

When I long for her to lay in my arms, that I can forever hold her tight, continually caress her all through a dreamy night.

And whenever she's near, it is as though spring is always in the air, and no matter what kind of fate that befalls me, I can feel no despair.

"Am I in Love?" Now that my skies are always sunny and bright, since she came into my life.

As I dream of her whether night or day.
Whereas each time I see her face, it makes me feel this way. Could it be a phase I'm going through, that has turned my gray skies blue.

Is it real, what I feel each time I lay eyes on her. One of my friends has said that she's just a witch with a pretty face.

Who has came up from hell, casting devilish spells, as if I may have been chased, But I beg the differ in this case.

When declaring that she is an angel, perhaps from the heavens above, from whence she fell.

Speaking words in a soft and gentle tone that brings me joy, whenever I hear the sweet sound that echoes within her voice.

Whereas it seems as though my heart spins with the zest of a carousel, whenever she appears, and comes into my atmosphere.

As her kisses and hugs, gives me such delight all of the time. And whenever I look upon her rare beauty, it blows my mind.

"Am I in Love"

In Eyes Of Tomorrow

In Eyes of Tomorrow," lies dreams and fortunes that have been quite untold, with gifts of treasures that are awaiting to be chose.

Where wishes and dreams can come alive, and blossom out of the night, with vibes to excite.

Where the colors of springtime shines with the early morning's light. If you are willing to compete, and refuse to give in to defeat.

That you may journey to the destination that awaits you. Where times may seem to get a little rough,

where you must stand tough. Only if you have the drive, and the fortitude,

to tackle the unforgiving challenges that lies ahead. That you may grab hold of success, by giving your best.

Lift up your head, and hear what is being said. As you might have been feeling down and out.

Confused about the route that you must take to get on the right track, when wandering in doubt, with the winds at your back.

Feeling as though you might have been living in a mixed up world, that is hard to fathom.
But don't give up, merely hold on tight, keeping the goals of your future within the rim of your foresight.

Along with integrity, and courage that rises high, when keeping your eyes on the prize, gazing beyond the distant sky.

Grab hold of a strong mentality, then be vigilant. Just as the light of the sunrise breaks out from the stormy weather.

Let go of any sorrow, that may linger as a part of you. But if not for today, then maybe,
"In Eyes of Tomorrow."

Which can relieve you of worries. When the sky is fresh with early morning sunshine,
as a new day begins to unwind.

Don't give in, casting your cares to the winds. Press on, straight ahead, and don't be afraid.

Accept whatever good, you may get out of life. Then throw down, with what you have gotten, and persevere, until your time comes around.

Letting nothing deter you from the correct path of life, that lies ahead. Be of good cheer, and of goodwill instead.

Let your decisions be clear and precise, for fighting a good fight, and never let negative vibes be your guide. When in each of our lives some rain must fall, that it wash away what we perceive as a bother.

So that the dark clouds can let go of the sun. that it may shine. If not for today, then maybe, "In Eyes of Tomorrow."

Where yesterday crawls into the sky, and fads away. When a new beginning is ushered in, springing alive as time goes rolling by.

For this is the way the pattern of life will sometimes go, till sunny days lines up in a row, beaming before your curious eyes.

Putting on a magnificent show, with a big surprise of wonder and delight, giving you a smile with wisdom to be wise.

As the start of a new day is refreshed by an early morning sunrise, that zaps away the darkness that may lie before your curious eyes, as you continue to strive.

Invigorating your mind with whatever is fair and true. Banishing the doubts that you may cling to, as you go wandering about.

As the fires of dawn burns out of the night, that your dark days may beam sunny and bright.

As your journey through life may appear to be gloomy at times, may feel as though you are falling behind.

But be that as it may, things are prone to turn around, at the break of dawn, and before the evening sun goes down.

When the morning sun of a new day will began to rise, eliminating the burdens of your bother.

When your future may take wings and fly, beyond the distant sky, more then you may ever realize.

"In Eyes of Tomorrow."

THE MONKEY CAGE

It was soon after the break of dawn, when the light of the early morning sun had just begun to rise on a tropical island.

Shedding light on a man named Okater Duesun, who was seen riding in a tall wagon pulled by a team of wild horses.

Whereas the animals had eagle feathers extending from the crown of their heads, fluttering roundabout their ears as it would appear.

When the wagon was loaded with stacks of long iron rods, and steel bars in which Okater collected. As the items had been abandon and discard.

Whereby the horses were huffing and puffing as they made their way, struggling to get across the rough terrain before the ends of day.

When Okater had a hold on the extended reins, as he was guiding, and controlling the team of four legged animals.

When clinging to a snakeskin whip that he would sometime use, when feeling the need to strike the animals that they may pickup speed, let their hooves rip, as they proceed.

When the eagle feathers were fluttering lightly within the winds, as he would yank the reins that curled beneath the horses chins, when calling out for them to obey.

Forging ahead as the animals were led. With the eagle feathers clinging to the crown of their heads as they made their way from a volcanic island without delay.
"Get on up there! You mangy old animals, and move it out!

Faster! Faster! Faster!" You could hear the man say,

as he would strike a blow with the whip, snapping it only within the winds. When yelling out demanding words time-and-time again.

Trying to hurry back to his commune as he traveled along the way, back to the newly found green grassy land.

Where he, and the people of the commune had begun to live, clinging to a different kind of survival plan that would require more of a skill.

Whereas the long black iron rods, and steel bars that were being hauled within the wagon, hooked up behind the team of wild horses as they were being pulled along.

Were to be used in the construction of a large holding pen, where wild animals were to be retained, trained, and remain.

When captured by the man called Okater, and others who lived within the commune, as time would resume.

It had been more then a year since the last volcano erupted on the vacant island, from whence Okater had obtained the iron rods and steel bars.

Whereby you could still see shadows of thick black smoke, billowing from the top of the volcano's fiery crater, which would still exist, and continue to persist.

However since that particular time the people found another place to live, a hidden island that had been recently revealed.

As they would soon pack up their belongings, when fleeing to the new found grassy land where they began to stay.

Where more viable vegetation exist as they made their way.
Known as the Island of Gulls, where seagulls and other birds gathered in heaps.

An area where the food was plentiful as the birds would go there to nestle and eat, where the valleys would run steep.

And where the world's most largest gorillas would live and grow, when at the beginning of nightfall, you could hear some of the hairy beasts when they began to roar.

Whereas in this hemisphere men would hunt these great apes for the use of their body parts, and also for the use of their thick black fur.

Where in other parts of the world unauthorized sales would occur. Men would also capture some of the huge gorillas when putting them inside a tall bamboo fence,

supported with barbed wire panels. Covered with sheets of tin where the animals would be locked within.

Teaching them how to obey when training them to heed to their demands, as they were trying to make them understand how to carryout the scope of a plan.

Whereby the man who was the owner, and trainer of these remarkable animals would beat them, and punish them.

When trying to make them do fancy tricks. A bloody design that had been taken out of the darkest pages of time.

Match them up with other gorillas in a death match, to rumble in the night, when they would be thrust into bloody fights.

As a sport for wagering bets, and for the people delight.
Whereby Okater would lock the large beasts inside an enclosed bamboo fence, where the height of it was immense.

When keeping the animals there for days, teaching them how to do tricks and how to behavior. When carrying out the events in which they would be engaged.

Then when performing their tricks, and when the gorillas were to be involved in a death match. The animals would be put into a large steel pen,

which was known as "The Monkey Cage." Where large bets were placed and money was made. Based on which beast would win, continue to survive when the other would die.

It was during one late afternoon, when Okater, who owned most of the gorillas. Would stage an event where all the inhabitants from around the island would attend.

To see the hairy animals do their tricks, engage in bloody death matches. As they would rumble and tumble from the ends of daylight, over into the darkness of night.

That they may sustain the existence of their lives. As they would battle one another to stay alive, when thrust into a fight where they would live or die.

Whereby some of the baboons, and chimpanzees would have to perform their tricks before the beginning of a death Match. During their fancy tricks when getting in the mix.

Standing on their heads, dancing, and playing dead. Jumping through hoops, flipping over and over again, doing a trick called the loopy loop.

However when the death matches would take place inside the compounds of the tropical grounds, some of the baboons,

and chimps would be playing above "The Monkey Cage."
Swinging and watching from the top of the surrounding tall green trees.

Within the commune where they sometime played as if in a maze. Swinging back and forth munching on some of the hanging leaves.

When on this particular night people would gather in heaps. To see the bloody death match scheduled to take place between the gorilla known as Cojo, and his opponent.

Who went by the name of Lomax, a huge gorilla. The largest anybody had ever seen, when he was just as mean.

In a fight to the finish, that was set to take place inside "The Monkey Cage." Where one of the beasts must die, and the other would continue to live with a good chance to survive.

Soon a group of men would bring Cojo out of his holding pen, from the confines of the bamboo barbed wire fence.

That set inside thick brush and tall trees where he was held captive, ever since his arrival, as he struggled for survival.

Soon he would be led into the "The Monkey Cage," coming in from the rear gate locked in chains as he came.

Whereas he would violently howl and growl, as the men led him over to the cage when being restrained.

When the trainer, Okater, had shocked and harassed the huge animal. That he may be annoyed, made to be vicious and mean, the way it was meant for him to be seen.

As the animal would roar with a loud voice. To get the people stirred, by the furious sounds and emotions that they had witnessed and heard.

As onlookers would sat and wait as they were thrilled, and began to cheer when the huge gorilla would appear.

Soon the other gorilla would be led into "The Monkey Cage," also locked in chains, when treated exactly the same. Shocked and harassed before he came.

Then suddenly the man who would conduct the death match would began to callout. "Men and women! Girls and boys! Hear the sound of my begging voice!

Welcome to 'The Monkey Cage!' Where tonight two gigantic man eating gorillas will fight to the death, as you please.

Where one will live, but the other must die. And this fantastic death match will be taking place right before your eyes!"

The man would shout out, wearing a tall black hat, black coat, and a red suit, with black boots rising up to his knees.

"Loose the chains! And shut the steel gates!" The announcer would yell and say. When a large gate had been put in place as it fell, and another had been slammed shut as it shall.

Then there! Right then and there, the two huge animals would clash, as they began to fight. Grunting and groaning, with madness on their faces when the battle was raging.

Rumbling in the night with no despair, inside the steel cage as the onlookers would intensely gaze, when dust and other debris were flying into the vapor of the air.

And from the hollow of the animals mouths, wet saliva was flinging out and about, as the people sat and stare.

Where flaming torches that had been placed roundabout were blazing with huge reddish flares, giving hazy light to the darkness of night.

Then as time was moving right along, one of the large gorillas would fall. when he had been slammed down hard, as if his huge body had shook up the ground.

When the beasts were tossing each other around, up and down right from the start, trying to tear one another apart.

Then there, the blood soaked body of the gorilla who went by the name of Lomax would lie still.

When you could hear him loudly breathing, as he would take his last breath, which appeared to be unreal.

Then there he bled, where soon he would lay dead with one of his paws resting across the forefront of his head.

Whereas the beast that was known as Cojo had survived, managed to stay alive when the other beast would die.

And as the death match had came to an end, Cojo would growl, and beat upon his hairy chest, then let go a loud roar in victory. In a show of bravery that all the people may know.

Then as time swiftly moved along such types of death matches would continue, as these magnificent animals would be killed, have their blood spilled, misused and abused.

However, there came a time when Cojo the fighting gorilla, would be allowed to mate with a female gorilla, who was named Lucill.

That the two of them may have a little cheer, when the desire appeared to be burning within their will.

Soon the female gorilla, would give birth to a baby boy gorilla who was named Surmoan. Whereas Okater, the owner of Cojo, was also the owner of Surmoan the baby gorilla.

Then as a small amount of time had gone by, and when the baby gorilla had grown somewhat bigger and stronger, after being nurtured by its mother, Lucill.

Okater would began training Surmoan, the baby gorilla,
to become a death match fighter, that he may someday fight inside "The Monkey Cage." Where bets and heap of money was made.

Whereas Cojo, the daddy gorilla was not happy with what his eyes could see. Whereby he begun to misbehavior, acting up in ways that seemed to demonstrate that this could not be.

Then in the process of time there was an uprising. When a strange woman went lurking around the holding pens, during the night when the event of a death match fight was about to begin, and get underway. When the onlookers had gathered around still trying to settle down.

Whereas the strange woman would get a front row seat, when sitting cross legged. Wearing a short red dress that would rise just above her thighs, with the wink of an eye.

When wearing a red lipstick smile, and splashing tantalizing perfume about her head and shoulders, repeating the trend over-and-over again.

Which certainly had an effect on the savage beasts in a sinuous way. As she was playing the harlot whether night or whether day.

Then on the very next morning the sun would rise up, right on time, overlooking the island with a show of sunshine.

When Cojo, and two other gorillas would break out of their holding pens, to free themselves from their captivity.

Found a way to escape from the barbed wire holding places, where they were held inside an area of thick brush and tall green trees.

Cojo would go in search of the strange woman which he had laid eyes on, during the night of the last deadly fight. As the two other gorillas who escaped would go tagging along.

Soon the animals were able to find the woman, when tracking her down, tracing the scent of her tantalizing perfume that she splashed about. When she was hanging around waiting to see what was going down as time played out.

Suddenly there she stood, awaiting at the edge of a nearby wooden shack, at the end of a secluded dirt road. When Cojo would slowly approach the woman.

Growling, and grunting, beating upon his chest, moving back and forth when tramping upon the fallen leaves. With his long hairy arms dangling down past his knees.

When he, and the other two gorillas had managed to make their way out of a tall patch of trees.

And when the woman laid eyes on Cojo, she would callout to him. "What do you want from me? You great big boy, of a dirty old ape.

Tell me, what can I do for you tonight, big boy? Can I turn your dark days bright?" She would say with a smile upon her face, as she began slowly walking towards Cojo.

Then suddenly you could hear the ravens in the background, wailing when the night was failing.

When your eyes could see flaming torched burning with a glow, as men were making their way when on the go. During a strange period of time when the four winds would suddenly began to blow.

As the sound of barking dogs, and wild horses could be heard coming in the night. When the hooves of the horses were pounding the ground, beneath the pale moonlight.

Whereas Okater, the owner and trainer of the fighting gorillas, along with some of his men had setout on horseback earlier that same day. Riding the animals when chasing the apes, with a pack of wild dogs leading the way. As they were soon upon the three gorillas sometime after sunset.

Carrying large heavy nets, in a quest to track the animals down, trap them with their heavy nets to bring them back, to be exact.

And when the pack of wild dogs came upon the three runaway gorillas, barking and gritting their teeth.

The savage beasts would reach down and grab hold on a few of the dogs, pick them up and bite into their flesh. Penetrating the dogs bodies with their huge sharp teeth.

Then with their brute strength they flung them across the way, as the three huge apes tramped upon the wild dogs, whereby the beasts would move out without delay.

Nevertheless, Okater along with a few of his men would soon recapture the animals using large and heavy nets, as they would return them back into their holding pens.

Then as time passed, one late foggy tropical night, when the moon was shinning with the paleness of light.

As the people were fast asleep inside their bunkers and wooden huts. There would come a man who went by the name of Jumbo Ellit.

Who was a friend to the animals, and wanted to see them protected and never neglected. Who had sympathy for the death match gorilla who was known as Cojo.

He also wanted to see the young gorilla named Surmoan, be excluded from the training that would make him a death match fighter. A dilemma he had protested.

Then as time went by, Jumbo Ellit could not get any cooperation from the owner/trainer, Okater Duesun, to set the animals free. When on a dark and foggy night,

when the moon was void of light. Jumbo would disguise himself when painting his face, and at a fast pace he would race to the location of the commune.

Where he would quietly creep across the grassy grounds of the wide open commune. With a silver dagger hanging from his waist, when moving about in haste.

As he would use the silver dagger when cutting into Okater's awaiting hut. Then there, he grab hold of the trainer as the man was fast asleep, could not hear a peep.

Jumbo would then quickly strike the trainer about the head, with a weapon that was found lying near the man's bed, when knocking him out.

Quickly and quietly he would pull Okater out of his sleeping quarters, and out of the enclosure of his wooden hut.

When quietly and in haste, he would drag the ruthless man across the commune grounds. Making way to the tall steel Monkey Cage,

and when he arrived there. He tossed the man across his shoulder, and carried him through the steel gates. Then there, he would lay the man down, inside the belly of the cage.

Where he would strike the trainer once more about the head, as the man lay on the dirty ground where blood stains could be found.

Then swiftly, Jumbo would make way, go into the tall bamboo fence and bring Cojo out from his holding place. Lead the beast over to "The Monkey Cage."

And when he arrived near the gates, he led the gorilla inside the cage. When there he tried to remove some of the broken chains from the beast, that partially bounded him.

As he would quickly go back outside the cage, and lock the large steel gates. Couldn't be late, as time would not wait.

Suddenly Okater, the trainer, would regain conscious and open his eyes. When there! The tall gorilla was standing towering over him, staring down at the trainer with his big bloodshot eyes. Then quickly, as in fear the trainer raised up and stood on his feet. As he gazed about looking for a way out.

When he began running around inside the cage. As if trying to break loose and set himself free, but it was not meant to be.

As the animal slammed the man back down into the dust of the ground, where the man laid stretched out on the blood stained floor of the cage, the second time around.

Then when the trainer looked up once again, there stood Cojo, The daddy gorilla still locked in some of his broken chains, as he had madly came. Growling and howling.

When suddenly, Cojo, would grab hold of the man once more, and whip him about, breaking some of his bones, as you could hear Okater when he began to moan and yell out.

Suddenly the huge gorilla slammed the trainer hard, back down into the dust of the ground. Where the man bled, and right then and there he would lay dead.

Then the rain came, falling upon the trainer's face, as he lay dead inside the blood soaked cage, where his broken body would remain.

Soon Jumbo Ellit, the friend of the animals would assist the gorilla known as Cojo, help him get away and escape back into the wild.

When Cojo, along with the female, Lucill, and the baby gorilla, Surmoan. Would live together happy and free,

in a safe place for the rest of their days. As it was long overdue, and perhaps, it was meant to be.

"The Monkey Cage"

BLOWING KISSES

The end of New Year's Day was upon us. When all the parties, and celebrations of song and dance had came to a close.

When once again it was time for the both of us to depart, and go our separate ways. After spending time together for the last few days.

Pack our begs and hit the road, when our sad goodbye seemed to have put a break in our hearts right from the start.

As the wonder of our togetherness had begun to fade, moments after our last embrace. Which had taken place just before we were out bound, as departure time had been announced.

When we would embark upon our out going journey, back to our designated places, with a smile playing upon our faces.

As we began "Blowing Kisses" back and forth, which flies in both directions, as they would twist and spin within the winds.

When we would be standing just beyond the doorway of the departure facility, as we began to go our separate ways.

"Blowing Kisses" that float on air, of a love so true that none can compare. When during so would relieve some of our despair, that we would sometime share.

When saying so long, then in a flash we were off and gone.

During moments of times when our lips could not meet, and the kisses that were blowing in the winds,

turned out to be soft and sweet. A small token of our love, which would carry over until our journeys were complete.

When we shall meet again, wishing upon a shooting star that our togetherness,

will never end, and that the love we have for one another will somehow reach out farther.

As we would be looking back when walking away, turning our heads around as we gaze into each other eyes by no surprise.

Blowing the kinds of kisses that holds together precious memories, which thrives deep down inside our hearts.

Memories that we can never discard, that keeps our hearts warm, a trait to be conformed.

As winter would sometimes wait just beyond the door, as it has done many time before.

"Blowing Kisses," as soft as the winds, for the love we would be missing, when leaving on a night train, or taking flight aboard a jet plane.

As our imagination leaps back into the past, whenever we are departing, going through a change.

Thinking about the wonderful times we had when our destinations were the same.

During the time when we lived side-by-side, in the same neighborhood beneath the open sky.

Until that period of time came to an end, changed course and ran out, dismissing the way things had been.

Wishing we can live near one another once more, perhaps we should, if only we could.

Which brings back thoughts of sweet romance that we have often known, as time has shown.

By the love we share as we truly cares. In hopes that it would last forever, as time would go dragging along.

Blowing the kinds of kisses that we embraces, with thoughts of a warm and passionate love affair, as such.

When our lips could not touch, as we went our separate ways for so many days.

When all we could do were blow kisses in the winds, when we were departing, as our togetherness would come to an end.

Kisses that are induced by the goodbyes we sometimes say, whenever we would go away.

Sojourn to the regions in which we would tread, by the hands of destiny as we are led.

Whenever we are separated for a period of time, whereby romantic fantasies penetrates our minds.

That our love affair be held together, and
continue to grow and stay, of a love we misses.

By the kisses that went blowing in the winds. Till we
meet again, on another day.

"Blowing Kisses"

When The Jay Bird Sing

It was an unforgettable period within the city, and within other surrounding cities of the region. Where ruthless men would often lurk,

sneaking about when carrying out their dirty works, for unlawful reasons anytime of the seasons. Prowling to and fro across state lines during a specific time.

When the streets were plagued by criminal activity. Where violence, and burglaries were on the rise, as a host of unscrupulous men were trying to get by, working their schemes by any means as a way to survive.

Men who were living raw, outside the boundary of the law. Some who had a knack for ripping off fancy automobiles,

and hot diamonds in ways that seemed unreal. In relation to a life in which they were chasing, when misbehaving as the yesteryears would reveal.

When roaming the streets of the city as they would constantly do, on various occasions. Seeming to be quite aggressive when indulging in their criminal behavior.

Searching for bogus ways to survive, hiding out in secret places when trying to stay alive, bringing their female counterparts along just for the ride.

Looking for ways to scratch out a dishonest living inside the city, once known as TeleBay Peaks, a city that thrived and would never sleep. As the men would exhibit ruthless persuasion when engaging in criminal behavior. Hustling and bustling, going to and fro as if no one would ever know.

Creeping roundabout, during the better part of a day. Fast women and thuggish men, clinging to the kind of life which they knew was not right, to fulfill the vow of their blight.

When trying to get away without the shadow of a doubt, running wild in the streets trying to figure things out.

Rendezvousing in devilish places that shined with neon lights, smoky places in the darkness of night where whisky was consumed in a downstairs private room.

Where they could reconvene to draw up their bogus plans and clever schemes, which only they could understand, in defiance of the rule of law, when living raw.

Doing things their way, running about night and day, hanging out in secret places where they would sometime play.

Where the violent men would get into fights, rumbling and tumbling deep into the night. When wicked women would be there for their delight.

Where uncontrollable chaos was raging, and the lawless men who had a craving for the big money,

and for pretty women to be their honeys, would constantly drink the wine of greed, members of a ring of thieves.

Getting drunk on the idea that stolen money and hot diamonds would set their minds at ease, that their quest for happiness may be appeased.

Where corruption ran deep within the hearts of men, as if beasts of the wild, when roaming the streets of a concrete jungle hunting for prey to make a kill.

When wearing a disguise, setting a dangerous trend where blood would be spilled as men die, for the hunter to live.

As violence and mayhem was running ramped by swindles and thieves, for their unlawful misdeeds to be achieved.

Along with con artists, and pickpockets that were roaming the streets of the city, where the lights were semi-bright, when moving through the dead of night.

As they were on the prowl hunting for easy prey, someone who might have been slowly moving about when on display.

Where at certain times they would chase the prey down, then devour it with scheme and scams, trapping it with a sham. Men and women who were living as beast of the wild, as if you could hear them howl.

Whereby their humanly prey would occasionally be killed, that the hunters may get their thrill no matter who would die, which would definitely occur once in awhile.

Member of a criminal enterprise, who would never be satisfied. As they would be out prowling about, hunting for easy prey, whether night or whether day to make you pay.

Then in the process of time, a certain group of these outlaws of men and women would come together, for an unlawful cause with money on their minds, which they would setout to find at any given time.

Determine to form an illegal operation known as the Money Club, to feed the jaws of their greed, do as they please.

Clinging to tricks and trades that were meant to deceive, when the cops classified them as just a ring of thieves.

Where in certain parts of the city they would make their rounds, when prowling the streets of downtown.

Where they were boosting, and peddling hot items as profitable goods. Doing whatever they could to siphon off your funds, threatening with big guns to get the job done.

The group was made up of men and women who held regular jobs, but who were also involved in the operation of a criminal enterprise, that was destine to be dissolved.

A multimillion dollar business, in cahoots with the black market which operated on the down low. Consisting of auto theft when they were on the go, taking and selling car,

along with other types of automobiles. Staging accidents when ripping off insurance companies, when the facts were unclear, keeping their intentions concealed.

Selling guns to other outlaws, and to convicts who were on the run. Involved in diamond heists, perhaps once or twice on any given day whenever they could get away.

Taking items out of the heart of the city, along with the most lucrative diamonds that existed in some of the high rises,

and other facilities that operated downtown, where some of the most expensive diamonds would abound.

Ripping off the most expensive cut diamonds in which they referred to as hot ice, when pulling off the notorious diamond heists. Whether it was night, or inside the rim of daylight.

The law officers in the city would crackdown on some of the perpetrators, but could not completely bust up the ring of thieving thugs, as the cops preferred.

Since the criminals who were involved would often operate across state and city lines, most of the time.

Soon the police chief in the city of TeleBay Peaks, would call in the FBI, who would assist in the unusual case.

Launch an investigation in just a matter of days that could bust the illegal operation wide open, as they were hoping.

Where the criminal acts were being staged in secret underground locations, moving from place to place, robbing various cities blind when creeping through the aisles of time.

Then as the hard days kept rolling along, the FBI would come up with a strategy. Whereas they decided to setup an undercover sting,

in a quest to try and find a jay bird that was willing to sing.
Come up with someone who could assist them in putting a stop to the chaos. Find out the names of those who were responsible for getting men popped.

Whereas the law enforcement agents would arrest some of the players, who were entrenched in the prevailing details. Perhaps a person who was a part of the ring of thieves.

When searching for someone to discover a path that would lead them to the trouble, which was brewing undercover.

A participant who was willing to become an informant. A person that was not afraid to talk, who had been involved with the ring of thieves and could not be deceived.

Someone who knew what was going down in certain cities and across town, that they may bring word of what occurred.

Inside the illegal criminal enterprise of a business that was operating in disguise with something to hide, An informant who would sing like a bird, in an effort to extract valuable information in relation to what they had heard, during the times when the crimes emerged.

Delve into what they had seen, of an illegal business that was operating as a fine tuned machine, bumping along on the side trying to make stride.

Whereby the FBI and the police officers would place them under arrest, hope for the best that some of them may have a burning desire to confess.

Soon a police sting would get underway and be carried out. When some of the criminals that were apprehended would ultimately express,

involvement to the charges that had been levied against them, which would be analyzed and assessed.

Whereas others would cop to a plea, bargaining for a lighter sentence, or to pay a small fee as they hoped it would be.
Wherefore among these criminals, there existed a peculiar fellow who went by the name of Clio "Fat Cat" Bosezo.

Who began to talk, spewing information of smooth words, and tall tales that the cops had never heard. Making lots of fuss, singing like a bird,

rambling on and on when spilling his guts. About what had went down during the time the crimes occurred. When the FBI dubbed him the Jay Bird.

Due to the fact that he was willing to talk, in order to save his skin. Singing like a bird to all the surrounding lawmen, word-by-word, as they would listen and observe.

Pleading for a lighter sentence, in return for information that could bust the notorious criminal ring wide open.

Whereby the police chief, and the FBI, would use the man as a bird on a string. Allowed him to fly away into the night.

Prowl deep into the underworld till the break of day, with intentions to repeat this method perhaps twice a week when doing things their way.

Then they decided to reel the stool pigeon back in, as the week had came to an end. when the law enforcement agents were ready to make some of the arrests.

And get a conviction against the members of the illegal organization, in relation to their anticipation.

Since Clio "Fat Cat" Bosezo, the stool pigeon, had taken their advice, went undercover to see what he could discover. Trying to assist in bringing the criminal enterprise down, which was operating in the streets of downtown, and across various state and city lines during this particular time.

When he had been ordered by the FBI, and the police chief earlier. To go undercover and infiltrate the criminal ring,

where members were living by a secret code, when trying to stay in control of the criminal enterprise which they chose.

Come up with new evidence that would coincide with the evidence that the cops had found, when getting inside the business that was operating underground.

Gather information from members of the group that he could relate to, for a lighter sentence this is what he was told to do.

Then during the time when Fat Cat had gone undercover, people who were broadcasting the news would ask the police chief, and the FBI.

When would they make additional arrests to bring the ring of thieves in, that they may stand trial and be brought to justice.

"When the Jay Bird Sing," the law enforcement agents would say. When referring to Clio "Fat Cat" Bosezo. Who was being used as a bird on a string.

When he had gone undercover as an informant. A man who was said to be just a pawn in a deadly game, as it remained.

The cops stated that Fat Cat, would sing like a bird, with evidence of information which they had never heard, of criminal activity that had recently occurred.
Then as time progressed, Clio "Fat Cat" Bosezo, whom the cops had dubbed the Jay Bird. Had been kidnapped by members of the criminal enterprise.

Whereby the underground organization accused him of singing like a bird to the cops, spilling his guts when refusing to stop. That the stool pigeon must die, setup to be popped.

Nevertheless, when the law enforcement agents did not hear from Fat Cat, for a day or two after time had gone by.
As he had been taken for a ride.

Since the time in which he had gone undercover, in a quest to assist the cops in shutting the illegal racket down, that operated underground.

The agents had decided to take action, go in and make a bust on certain facilities that were occupied by some of the ring leaders, and other suspects.

During a time when the gang of criminals would not be expecting a bust to be staged. But the FBI contended that they, in due time.

Would only facilitate the bust with a well thought out raid. When the perpetrators were not expecting a raid to take place, when all the law officers were in agreement.

Whereas they would begin retracing the steps of the perpetrators, that would take place in a matter of days in differing ways.

Then they would infiltrate the places where arrests were to be made, and take the ring of infamy outlaws down.
But only during the time, "When the Jay Bird Sing." With new information that would assist them in the manner of their undercover operation, for bringing down the criminal ring.

Be that as it may, it was learned that Clio "Fat Cat, the stool pigeon, had freed himself from his captors. Got away after some delay.

When he would telephone the FBI agents and other law enforcement officers. When there! Right then and there, he would began to sing like a bird.

Advising the law enforcement agents of the evidence he had found, that could be collected from the business which was operating underground.

Out of buildings belonging to the suspects, places that the outlaws could not protect. The FBI, along with other law enforcers would pull together,

and map out all the places within several cities to be hit at the same time, when the raid would unwind.

As they readied themselves with sophisticated weapons that were the best, dressed in dark uniforms with riot gear, wearing bullet proof vests.

To carryout a raid that the ring of thieves could not resist, that would not be dismissed. Employing a strategy that was destine to succeed.

When the officers would converge upon the buildings where various members of the illegal operation would surrender peacefully, as the enforcers would insist.

However other would engage in a shootout, without a doubt. As the cops would hunker down behind trees and automobiles. Where men were killed, and blood was spilled.

As the criminal enterprise was eventually brought down, when it was illegally operating underground in various cities and towns.

Thanks be to the FBI, the city law enforcement officers, and other government agencies. Also thanks be to the man who went by the name of Clio "Fat Cat" Bosezo.

Who was also responsible for taking out the deadly operation of the illegal organization, as time went by. When shootouts had occurred as men were arrested and others had died.

Whereas some of the participants of the underground criminal ring would be convicted, as they would stand trial.

When other would be killed during a successful police sting, that innocent citizens may do the right thing to survive, and stay alive.

When others who were caught up in a bad deal, before the word was revealed, in reference to the sting, would be able to recover, move forward and continue to live.

"When the Jay Bird Sing"

To God Be The Glory

Give thanks for the rising sun, when the day has begun, and for the stars and the moon that shines pearly bright.

Filling the sky with an array of perfect light, before the morning is visible to your eyes.

As the heavenly bodies gently radiate far and wide, throughout the darkness of night.

When shining as diamonds in the sky, creating a heavenly site by the power of the Almighty.

Who continue to bless the world with all necessities. That you can be pleased, and that you may believe.

Gives you rest from worry and stress, guides you through the path of peace, when on the right accord to maintain dignity and joy.

That you may not be obsessed with the ways of the world, practices that may lead you astray.

"To God be the Glory," and by his word of truth you must strive to obey. Live for the good of his blessings each and everyday.

As some would have you to believe, that the ways of the world holds the standards to which you must live. Claiming that it will suit you best. When in reality its suitability may be far less,

than what your mind has been led to believe. By the doctrines of the world which is not just a wild guess.

Something you may have to avoid, in a world that is prone to deceive, that you may not succeed.

Wherefore only through the love of the Almighty, can you be blessed of all things that are moral and holy, "To God be the Glory."

Of all things that are fair and true. Life giving waters, and fruits for the soul, of love that never grows cold.

That you live and thrive, by the genuine love that only the Almighty can provide.

Of the heavenly deeds that are wholesome and good, that are not to be misunderstood.

Be thankful for all things that are worthy of God's love, for the life giving earth that brings forth vegetation, of a divine revelation.

By his deliverance, of the wonders in which his love is revealed, and his goodness acclaimed.

That falls from the heavens above with power to heal, for the life he gives to be sustained.
That we grow, and thrive within the light of his blessings, which must always be maintained.
Coinciding with the sunshine and the rain.

For when you lean on him there is no need to be discouraged, when giving thanks for all his divine kindness. "To God be the Glory."

Wherefore he has all the healing power within his hands. For when you are sick, feeling down and out as if you can't get well.

He will comfort you, give you the strength and courage that will carry you through, when life seems uncertain and blurry.

As if you can't work things out, seem to be tossed about. Thereby your mind may be weary, and full of doubt.

When you are feeling as though you have done your very best, but cannot find the will and strength to carry on.

Then call upon his name, and he will give you rest, that the will of your mind may be strong.

And when it seems as though the burdens of the world are upon your shoulders, and cannot ceased.

When troubles just won't leave you alone, and the struggle for survival won't let you be.

No matter of the category, call on him, and he will give you peace, that your burdens be relieved, "To God be the Glory."

Then whatsoever you may try and do in life, strive to be true. whereas throughout the universe his love abides,

as sure as the light from the moon and the stars, which never cease to shine.

When decorating the night sky, far and wide, high and low. As the celestial bodies shines and glows, before the spirit of your soul.

Arise, and sing praises unto his name, and be of good cheer, and of courage that remains.

When at certain times his blessing burst forth in a flurry, when coming together, for his love endures forever.

"To God be the Glory"

An Echo Of Love

I can hear "An Echo of Love, flourishing from the sounds of sweet music,

that fills the springtime air, when love is in full bloom, as nothing else can compare.

Awakening some of the amusing thoughts, and laughter that will see me through, meditating on moments that I've shared with you.

Persuading me to relax, as my whole world seems to be brand new, as a matter of fact.

When my mind began reminiscing of the many fun things we often do, whenever we are together, even if days of just a few.

Bringing back colorful memories, that spring forth and began dancing within my head.

When "An Echo of Love," began moving to the pace of my heart beat, and to the rhythm of the four winds, as it spins.

Swirling around and around, whispering with a delightful sound. over-and-over again, never to be misled.

When I can feel the magic of the burning vibes that strays from you. when dispersing a few of your favorite love tunes. Into the thought patterns of my mind. That lends inspiration to the totality of my days, when the soft music plays.

With sound waves that glazes across the face of the howling moon, grabs hold of me real soon.

When I can feel "An Echo of Love," penetrating my heart, with the songs that my heart so often sings.

As it eases my aches and pains, when being without you, such a strain. Spinning with a distinctive sound when you are not around.

conveying the colorful sparkles that appears within your eyes, when dazzled by the beauty of the setting sun, upon your return.

Whenever you have gone to stay, if only for a short while, whether it be night or it be day.

As it gently pampers the vibration within the sounds of my ears, when opening my eyes.

To the reflections of bright and colorful images of you, turning my gray skies blue.

Echoing with wonder inside the walls of my mind with clarity, ranging with bits and pieces of yesteryear.

Whispering sweet melodies that creates such delightful memories, of moments I've spent with you, in days gone by.
That is soothing to me right from the start, with every beat of my heart. Keeping us together that we may never drift apart.

Then when I close my eyes, and you are not by my side. I can feel "An Echo of Love,"

softly touching me when you are away,

with lyrics that are sincere. Conveying that your love is for real, and shall never stray.

Blowing in the breeze with such an ease, over the mountains and across the seven seas.

As precious as the jewels of stars, that hangs from the bright constellations shining from high above.

Whispering with soft music, for only a spell, spinning with the zest of a carousel.

"An Echo of Love"

Pirates In The Sea
Of Black Pearls

The cold days of winter had just disappeared, fading away into the winds of the southern hemisphere.

When the refreshing days of spring had been revitalized. Soon to be spilling over into the summertime season, for all matters and reasons.

When a crew of men from Lake Providence, Louisiana. Took to the high sea in search of black pearls. When they would be accused of living their lives as pirates.

Simply because the men would climb aboard a large ship, as it was awaiting in the deep waters of the Mississippi river.

Whereas we had all signed up to shove off on a wild adventure, as we would travel the waters of the roaring sea, when there was no other place we would rather be.

In which we had trained, and prepared for such dangerous exploration, which had became a part of our expectations.

Then during this point in time, we were about to set sail, ready to hit the deep water trail. On a long and rugged sea trip, which was not just a hop and a skip.

As we would be sailing the deep waters of the ocean blue,
in which we were destine to do, to see the venture through.

That we may journey to an island that was once known as Tanzis, near the border of Tahiti. Which had recently signed onto a friendship treaty.

A place where magic radiates from the moon glow, just above the warm coastal waters where a multitude of diamond head oysters would appear, year-after-year.

When the summertime season was near, where oysters would nestle in the deep coastal waters during a certain period, when the stars were shining crystal bright.

Where the magic of the moonlight would flow, whenever the time was right, on a warm Polynesian night.

Whereas during the summertime season, the magic of the moonlight would hang just above the crystal waters, known as the Sea of Black Pearls.

Wherefore legend has it that during a certain period of the year during summertime. That the magic of the moonlight, was known to radiate during the height of a summer night.

When thousands upon thousands of diamond head oysters, would also nestle within the waters of a blue lagoon, that thrived beneath the light of a silvery moon.

During the period of a warm Polynesian night, when the pearls would be touched by the magic of the moonlight.

Where the blue lagoon would branch out from the South Pacific, where some of the most finest black pearls, in the whole wide world could be found.

It was late one summer evening when we set sail, guided by a man who called himself Capt. Hawk Eye. Who claimed that during this journey, we would be referred to as pirates,
by suspicious minds, in just a matter of time.
Simply because we were men boarding a large ship, known to have set sail toward the Sea of Black Pearls. With images of two fire eating dragon on our flag, flying in the winds,

as our voyage would began. When the captain would somehow be in charge, and be our guide. When two of my uncles, three of my brothers, and two cousins were on board.

Along with a group of other fellows who lived in, and around the city, who would also come aboard. Whereas we had all been trained, and prepared for the journey of a lifetime.

Then as we had embarked upon the large ship, shoved off and set sail, Capt. Hawk Eye would get everyone's attention.

That he may give the crew a motivational speech. which no one wanted to hear, telling us what to expect.

When he would be pacing back and forth across the moist wooden desk, as we were sailing aboard the wavering ship.

When we never knew the kind of words he would blurt out, as he began to speak, when most of us would gather around.

During a time when the ship's horn would blow with a loud sound. A signal for us to settle down, and give the captain our undivided attention in which he would seek.

"Men! Listen up! And hear what I have to say, people are known to die, for one reason or another, each and everyday.

Now if for any reason, someone should fall dead aboard this ship. No one must cry, but if any of you do,

don't hesitate to wipe the tears from your weeping eyes," the captain boldly said as we were advised and led.

"Now men!" The captain would continue to speak, when he was soon interrupted by one of the shipmates, who were standing near, lending an ear.

"But captain! You are suppose to be giving a motivational speech, to pump the men up, encourage them to go forward.

Not to remind them that they may die, we are referred to as pirates," the man would speak out and describe, as he was standing close by.

"That is exactly what I'm doing, motivating the men," replied the captain. "Letting them know right up front,

that we don't want no crybabies on this ship," the captain would say, as he paused for a second or two. Then hastily,

started speaking out once again, as he was not through, and for quite awhile it had been as he would go on and on.

"Now ladies! Uh, excuse me. I mean men! Just a little slip of the tongue, you know, ha-ha-ha-ha-ha," the captain would laugh out and say, as he pretended to play.

"Now men! We are suppose to be pirates, as some folks have said. And now we have set sail on a journey that may be hard and heavy, and at times it can be dangerous and deadly.

Some of us may never return, and on the other hand. Some of you may have a little fun, with the females in which we may encounter, before it is all said and done.

If you know what I mean! ha-ha-ha-ha!" The captain would say and laugh out loud, when we had shoved off and were on our way.

As he was trying to explain certain mixed up facts, and other things, that our minds were suppose to retain, and keep track.

"But whatever troubles that may befall us," the captain would go on to say. "And whatever delays that may take place, we must never give in.

Stand fast and keep our faces to the wind, and don't look back. Whereas you have been trained and prepared for this journey of a lifetime.

And it is all up to you to complete this voyage, that it may turnout fine, a destiny in which we have been assigned.

As we travel through the mysteries of time. And if we follow our plan, with a steady hand, from every available man.

We shall certainly see things through, myself and all of you." The captain would explain, putting it simple and plain.

"Then upon our return back to Lake Providence, after our journey has been completed," the captain would go on to say.

"We will all be rich! With black pearls, that are worth millions of dollars clean around the world."

Then only at this particular point in time, all the men began cheering, thinking that they were on the verge of becoming rich, as the captain would insist.

However, Capt. Hawk Eye, only had one eye. Wherefore some folks claimed that he had lost the other eye in a barroom brawl.

Fighting among men who were short, stout, heavy and tall.
Others would claim that he lost his eye when sailing the seven seas. As he was once known as a pirate.

Sailing with a pack of wolves pretending to be men, but who were thieves, prone to deceive. When they were operating as cutthroat pirates, with misdeeds to be achieved.

During their youthful years, men who were headstrong and had no fear. Who burst onto the scene sometime ago, as far as anyone claims to know.

At a time when the captain began wearing a black patch about his face, to cover up the cavity of his missing eye, for the rest of his days.

Said he had turned his life around, took his head out of the clouds, came back down to earth. Planting his feet on solid ground, with blood of a pirate still running through his veins.

Some folks have said that the reason he was given the name of Hawk Eye. Is because he claimed that he could see, three times better with the one remaining eye,

than he could ever see with both of them. When it struck him as a total surprise, stating that with the one good eye,

he was able to read men lips, whenever they begin to talk. Spy miles across the open sea like a hawk, and watch the world go by, as it would whiz right past his one eye.
However we had been at sea for only a few hectic days from the time we set sail. when Capt. Hawk Eye had managed to drift off course, getting us lost.

When we accidentally sailed to a seaside city known as Dead Man's Town, where some of the people who had died at sea were often buried.

Something that was out of the ordinary, only meant for the fallen seamen who were considered for having their lives and services cherished.

Then some of us would soon lower several of our canoes down into the waters, jump into the small boats, and row ourselves to the banks of the seaside city.

Where inside the city, zombies were stirring about. Mysteriously moving around, rising up into the air and
coming right back down.

Twisting and turning in midair, near the top edges of various buildings. With long gowns covering their ghostly bodies,

extending from their heads and down beyond their toes. Within the midst of a purple haze as it flowed.

As if they were floating on air, where the winds would take hold of their long gray hair. Fluctuating the wild strands again-and-again.

That hung about their heads, and beneath their chins when rustled by the winds. As they appeared to be arguing at one another, sounding as if they were only making lots of fuss.

It was as though they could not see us, when we were moving about, and searching through the cobblestone streets trying to work things out.

In search of food and other supplies, anything that may have appeared to be eatable to the sights of our wandering eyes.

As our rations were running low, when we were steady on the go, in a mold to survive beneath the warm summer skies.

It was now approximately the seventh day at sea, as we were lagging behind, not as far into the voyage as we thought we ought to be at that particular time.

Then it was late in the evening when the fog had draped over the deep sea waters, slicing our visibility in half.

When once again our ship had drifted of course, due to Capt. Hawk Eye negligence. Where the wind soars.

When he could not see as well as he had claimed. Wherefore unto him, the distance, and pattern of his directions appeared to be the same.

Which he could not live up to his name. Whereby he had been given such name because of his keen eyesight.

Claiming that he could see three times as better with his one remaining eye, then he could ever see when he had both of his eyes.

In which it was said, that he lost his missing eye in a barroom brawl, or fighting with other pirates in the sea of Bathoal.

However, we would have to find our way back to the correct sea trail in which we had mapped out, for a guiding resource.
Get back on course, as we thought we could afford on a foggy night,

when sailing beneath the pale moonlight. Plying straight ahead as we were led by Capt. Hawk Eye, who was always waiting nearby.

Then suddenly, there appeared a ship flying a flag that was snapping, and cracking in the gusting winds.

That bore the image of an assault rifle, flying under the foggy skies, reaching way up high when moving close by.

Suddenly the men aboard the vessel began firing there rifles into the air, as our eyes could see fire from the guns flickering in the darkness of night.

"OK men! Lets turn this ship around and head back to Lake Providence, for a storm is arising, and there is just too much lightning up ahead," the captain said.

"But Capt. Hawk Eye, we are now a long ways out to sea. Too far to turn back, to be exact, and that is not lightning your eye may see.

But what it appears to be is gunfire, coming from the weapons of the men who are sailing the ship up ahead," one of the shipmates said.

"Firing their weapons in despair, whereby the glimmer of light that your eyes might have seen, is just a flare, with smoke rising into the air."

"You mean somebody is shooting at us?" asked Capt. Hawk Eye. "Yes sir captain!" yelled the man. As our flag with images of two dragons were flying high, beneath the sky.

"OK fellows! Sail straight ahead to the left, where we can zip right past that crazy old ship, and leave it far behind in a short span of time.

Get away and escape this melee," the captain would say.

"But captain! We will ram the oncoming ship,

if we go in that direction!" yelled another shipmate. "Veer to the right captain! That we may slip by," the man shouted, as gun smoke from the approaching ship was rising high.

"Affirmative!" yelled Capt. Hawk Eye. "Turn the ship to the right men! That we may leave that old ship behind, in just a matter of time."

Then as time progressed, at this exact moment we had been at sea for more than fifteen days, and with the speed of time, we would race.

When the men were hungry and tired, anxious to find a place to rest up at seaside. As we were moving to a steady pace, through the long nights and rugged days.

During a period when we began approaching the island of Tanzis, sailing straight into the Polynesian night, by the magic of the moonlight.

Suddenly, Capt. Hawk Eye would began to speak, and make an announcement. "Alright men! I can see that one of you have gotten us off course once more," he would yell out.

"No captain, We are in the waters near Tahiti, in the Sea of Black Pearls!" One of the shipmates would yell.

"Well I know that! I was only trying to see if you fellows were paying attention," the captain would say, near the ends of a long and hot day.

"I knew, for a fact, that I could certainly get you boys here. Simply because I have been sailing these here waters, since I was just a boy."

The captain would go on to explain, when at certain times he would say funny things. Laughing and talking when playing some of his silly games.

Then there we were, entering into our destination, as our eyes could behold pearly light illuminating across the sky.

Then as we gazed across the waters, there were many ships spread throughout the Sea of Black Pears.

Where you could see a few of the village women, as they swirled. Gathered beneath some of the palm trees at the edge of the coastline.

Having a good old time. Wearing short skirts, with reefs of red headdresses upon the hair of their heads.

Wearing strings of black pearls hanging from around their necks, with sparkling diamonds combined.

Dancing and twirling batons, that were sizzling with flames of fire. As golden light was illuminating against their faces, as they were doing their jigs on hilly places.
When dancing in open spaces on the banks of the blue lagoon, as we had arrived none too soon.

Where men were diving beneath the current, down into the waters from the top of their ships. Going down and coming up with sacks of black pearls,

as they plucked them from the floor of the sea. Some fighting among themselves trying to get more than their share.

Other made their way to the blue lagoon. Where thousands upon thousands of diamond head oysters nestled in the waters of the nearby lagoon.

Beneath the magic light of the Polynesian moon. Near the coastline of the South Pacific where men were firing off some of their guns,

celebrating the amount of black pearls in which they had acquired, by all the hard work they had done.

We would also come up with our share, as we had been diving for pearls more than three days straight, when time could not wait.

Diving part time in the Sea of Black Pearls, where we would also bring up gold bars from a deteriorated desk,

of a sunken ship that was buried beneath the waters as the day was late. And at other times we would dive deep into the blue lagoon.

As we would finish up with one site, then move on to another, beneath the light of the Polynesian moon.
Quickly moving onto a different place when the time was right, as we continued to dive through the dead of night.

After collecting the pearls, we would jump into our canoes and make way back to our awaiting ship.

Climb aboard, and spread what we had obtained across the deck. When there! We were awash in the golden light of black pearls, a gift from the sea, as it would be.

When we were bursting with jubilation, in anticipation of being rich. Then soon we would turn our ship around,

and set sail back towards the states, when gazing back at the fading sun just before the day was done.

However, late one night somewhere in the South Pacific, as strange as it may seem. Men who claimed to be members of a deep water Sea Patrol, would climb aboard our vessel,

and confiscate most of the black pearls that we had obtained.
Take parts of the gold bars, that we had brought up from the sea, as they came. Accusing us of being pirates.

Many of them cloaked with tattoos, and wearing ponytails, men who seemed to look the same, oh so strange.

When letting the wind out of our sails. Men with the look of hard days, and long rough nights etched on their faces,
Accusing us of sailing to the wrong places.

Being in violation of the high sea laws, they would claim. Contending that we were obligated to pay, said they could not allow us to get away. But as it turned out, these men were really the pirates. Operating for a state that was run by a tyrant.

Men who had the reputation as "Pirates in the Sea of Black Pearls," who were known to rob, steal, and kill.

Perpetrating a high sea crime against us, in just a matter of time, as they soon sailed away leaving our ship behind.

However during the return journey back home, captain Hawk Eye retreated to his small cabin. Where he would spend his time alone, during things on his own.

After the pirates had robbed us of our black pearls, and gold bars, when we thought we would be living large from the richness of our treasure.

Which we had obtained when working so hard, came a long ways fighting the winds and the rain. And the biting jaws of the huge waves, as we tried to maintain.

Then as days pressed on, we had made our way back to Lake Providence. Wherefore the journey at times had been a terrifying ordeal.

As we would climb into our canoes, and row ourselves back into the waters of Lake Providence. As we had reappeared.

Then as a couple of days had past, after arriving back home. Rumors would began to surface.

Claiming that Capt. Hawk Eye, had retained some of the black pearls and a few of the gold bars. In which he had hidden away only for himself.
Whereas he had recently gotten married to a young lady, in which he, was twice her age. Some folks would contend that he was being played.

Nevertheless, the captain would pass away perhaps one years later, due to mysterious circumstances surrounding his death, when he was buried at sea upon his request.

When it was said, that the captain had buried a large amount of black pearls, and parts of the gold bars that he had kept for himself, somewhere in the vicinity of Lake Providence.

Perhaps within the clear waters of the lake. However, soon after his death, his young bride moved to New York City.

Where she purchased two new homes, in the style of two-story houses, when she began living on her own. Got behind the wheel of two expensive automobiles,

and established a fancy boutique of a dress shop. Where she began living large in New York City, right from the start.

But be that as it may, men came in search of the lost treasure, time-and-time again. As they would dive beneath the clear waters of the lake, as it became a trend.

Even rummaging through the graveyard grounds, as they came in search of the treasure from miles around, from different parts of the world. But none of the treasure, could ever be found.

"Pirates in the Sea of Black Pearls"

LET'S FALL IN LOVE

Since the first time I laid eyes on you, it was plain to see, that you had the makings of a princess, and the face of an angel.

One of the prettiest girls my eyes had ever seen, as I would gaze. When you were a stranger to my eyes, a lady I began to admire.

As if you were on display, in the manner of a precious jewel, that sparkles with the kind of shine that never loses the worth of its stay.

Reflecting a rare beauty when awaiting nearby, as you were standing with such an elegant profile without words to say.

When I could feel your love vibes, oozing into my heart, as my craving for you began to rise.

Something I've never experienced before, when as of yet, we had never met.

Perhaps since the two of us were always on the go, but as time went by I was longing to do so.

Without any delays in the coming days, for it seemed that you were the angel of my dreams.

Someone who had materialized, and blossomed right before my very eyes. An occurrence that seemed to be unreal,
as if something out of a movie scene, when an angel would magically appear.

Wherefore I would like to stress the fact, that I realize your time is very important to you,

but before you walk away, there is one thing I beg to say. If you will, and if you may.

"Let's Fall In Love!" On such a romantic night, awash by the beaming rays, that radiates from the stars of light.

Where you will be my gal, and I'll be your guy. As the wings of spring awaits us, with lovely fragrance that laces the air, as the days are fair.

That gives way to soft summer showers. Which in return, gives new life to the bouquets that grow colorful, with a burst of wild flowers.

Whereas we may seize the kind of happiness displayed by two loving doves, which seems to stay together forever.

As they take to the sky, spreading their wings then began to fly, as if the both of them were the grand prize, in the sight of each other eyes.

Emphasizing the kind of love that will give us a thrill, when our compassion begins to thrive.

With a love that both of our hearts can feel. A renewing love that will continuingly revise.
Where we can dance within the dazzling glamour of a starry night, find romance when playing within the alluring moonlight.

Where I'll be your only prince, and you'll be my only princess, for all the world to see.

Indulging in a satisfying love that is for real,
as it will spring forth to be revealed.

Come forth and spring alive, giving birth to a new
dimension that we may fruitfully abide as time goes by.

Held tightly together by our genuine kisses, and by the
warmth of our endearing hugs.

As we take control of our destiny, that it may pan out
and stay, as it will never go astray.

Then at any moment in time, whatsoever you need I
will provide, and whatsoever you desire, I shall supply.

"Let's Fall In Love," as we will indulge in the kind of
love that was meant to last forever. The kind that will
be handed down from above.

Prolonged by a divine destiny that hangs within the
air, with a promise that we will be such a lovely pair.

And with every beat of our hearts, we will coexist as
two lovers, living as a unit of one.
Whereby a strong romantic feeling will confirm
that such a love must persist, when splashed by the
morning sun.

Wherefore it will be a honey kind of love, soft and
sweet, absent of any dishonesty, and without any
scheming deceit.

A candy kind of love, with a flavor that is sugary
sweet. As of a lollypop, or lemon drops,

with a taste of honey. When our nights will be cozy,
and our days will be sunny.

Whereby we can take a ferry, or climb aboard a fancy cruise line, at a precise time. Take a romantic trip to Paris.

Then there we can be married, touched by the magic of true love, enchanted by the twinkling stars above.

Then forever, we shall always be together, as if two doves, of perfectly blending feathers.

"Let's Fall In Love"

A Kiss For The
Last Dance

It was the end of a performance, put on by a female song and dance group, that had taken place down at a popular event center.

Where a host of spectators had shown up for the occasion. When only a certain number of guests, and fans were allowed to enter.

During a time, when "rock and roll" was here to stay. As some of the longtime fans of the singing group, were likely to remember.

Whether they could, or whether they may. As the women had finished doing their dance routines, and singing their popular songs, as they carried on.

With a fantastic band which played along. Rocking behind, keeping with the four beats of time.

Whereby the women would travel from city to city, putting on their intriguing shows as a form of entertainment.

When they would take to the stage, with the rhythm of a
fiery blaze. To do their fancy dancing and sing their songs.

As the spectators would steadily gaze, fixated on the group with a bird's eye view. when exhilarated and amazed.

The musical singing group consisted of four females, Carrie, Raven, Maxine, and Claresee. Who had came together as songbirds of a feather.
To create the fancy steps that were used in their dance routines, and to sing their songs of sweet melodies, that their fans would be pleased.

In which they called themselves the Shantells. As the recordings of their tunes had began to sell.

Whereby the nature of their performance would always turnout well, and based upon the perception of each appearance.

They would excel, and proceed to the top of the music chart for a moderate spell. Then at the end of the two shows in which they would perform.

When during each engagement beneath the glare of the spotlights, after being well received by the spectators, who were quite warm and polite.

The women had finished up, singing their songs, and doing their fancy dancing, when performing deep into the night.

When afterward, they would then take time, to go out into the audience, and mingle with the guests after their shows would come to an end.

Whether in a former gathering, a dance or concert setting, or a nightclub appearance, whatever the function had been.

Wherefore they would make themselves available to various men, the ones who had a wish to dance with them.

A privilege in which the men would certainly have a desire, where there was no reason to condemn.
As it was part of the contract agreement in which the Shantells had signed, that set forth a practice for the female entertainers to spend sometime with the guests.

Getting to know them, to build up their fan base, and gather followers that would recognize each face of the women, that they might keep pace with their progress.

The contract would also set forth, that the women have a little leisure time with the guests, when their shows were over and done, more or less.

That they may be accepted by the spectators and well-wishers. Whereas for these ladies it was not a big concern, as they would confess.

When convinced that they had the style and talent to standup to anyone, when it was all said and done.

Be that as it may, one of the clauses in the contract was a common practice, whereby the women would approach a man, whether an admirer or a fan.

Perhaps someone they may have wanted to befriend,
after their show would have came to an end.

Whereas a member of the female singing group may have walked up to a fellow. In which she may have been interested,

when she would propose, "A Kiss for the Last Dance," she would kindly say. Then she would take a step or two when moving in close, as she made her way.

When at the end of the party, or gathering. The DJ would make an announcement. "Ladies and gentlemen! This is the last dance for tonight.

So grab yourselves a partner and dance the night away, as the music begins to play," the DJ would loudly say.

However, during the last three months or so, when the
Shantells were performing in various cities.

There had been three homicides, which had taken place somewhere nearby. Within the circuit where the women would put on their shows, in cities that they had chose. Where men had been shot and killed by someone wheeling a 22-caliber revolver. A gun in which they would conceal.

In cities where the women singing group, had been performing during such times when the men had died.

Then on this particular bright night, the ladies would approach a few of their fans, with whom they had chosen to have a dance.

Prior to the last song to be played near the end of the gathering. "A Kiss for the Last Dance!"

The women would say to the men, as they came near unto them. When they would gently kiss the guys on their cheeks,

grab hold onto their hands, and lead them out onto the dance floor. Whereas the men would certainly be obliged,

dancing with the women in which they had a burning desire.
On such a gorgeous night, as the moon would be shining pretty and bright.

Then just about the time when the DJ was getting ready to spin one of their tunes. One of the members of the Shantells singing group,

whose name was Claresee Chenchillo. Would approach a man, who went by the name of Dorvon.

As he was standing alone, a man who would keep to himself most of the time, avoiding everyone else.

When he would setout, and go in search of places in which he would roam, by day or by night, at various times before returning to his home.

As he was eyeballing the woman when she was gracefully moving through the crowd, when the DJ was playing one of their favorite songs.

Which the speakers to the amplifiers were turned up quite loud, blasting out to the crowd. As the woman, Claresee, slowly walked up to the man, Dorvon, stared into his eyes.

When she would speak to him, "A Kiss for the Last Dance!"
She would propose, as she raised up, and began standing on her tiptoes. So that her lips could reach the height of his face,

when she had made her way through the place. As she would gently kiss the rather tall man on his cheek, took hold of his hand as she quietly led him out onto the dance floor.

When the lights were turned way down low, as the music would softly play. When the DJ began spinning the last song, as the night was late, and time would not wait.

Sending sound waves over the clarity of the amplifies, when the two would slowly dance cheek-to-cheek for quite awhile.

Till the end of the song would reach its peak. Then after the dance was over, together the two of them would walk away
hand-and-hand.

Making their plans as mates, at a very fast rate. As they would soon make their way to an area outside the city limit.

Where lovers would often go to rendezvous, in which most of the folks referred to the place, as lovers lane.

A place where people would go, those who thought their hearts were beating as one, playing the lovers game whenever they came.

Where Claresee, and Dorvon would get acquainted, and partake of each other's company, of pleasurable moments.

When the two of them had engaged in a casual manner of romance. Then when it was all said and done. Claresee would reach inside her handbag, and ease out a 22-caliber pistol.

Grab hold of the small gun, as she would raise it up, when the man head was turned. Whereas she would then take aim,

pointing the gun at the back of the man's head, as he was not looking. When she would pull the trigger. Pow! Pow! Shooting the man twice, claiming his life.
Then she would proceed by taking the money from his wallet, exit his vehicle and walk away, disappearing into the atmosphere of the following day without delay.

Then after this homicide had taken place, the cops would advise the community that a serial killer was on the loose.

Could be as many as one or two, as the officers were in the process of figuring out just what they were going to do.

What procedure to take, as they began to investigate. Come up with a strategy, to bring this murder mystery to an end.

Whereby a rough go into the case, it had already been.
As they were determined to see it through, and not pretend. Unravel the caper, where an unknown assailant,

had taken the lives of two other men. In a short span of time, something in which they would have to contend.

As the homicide task force, would soon get involved, when investigating the case, reeling various suspects in, as they were swiftly working at a steady pace.

Where within two months, three men had been found dead. When the killer, or killers had left behind the same MO.
Three times in a role.

Then as a couple of weeks had passed by, the female singing group would move on to another nearby city.

Where they had an engagement to perform at an auditorium on the night of a full moon, of Valentine's Day. When young lovers, and other fun seekers would come out to play.
Where the women would take to the awaiting stage, putting on their magnificent shows, until it was nearly time for the doors to close.

When soon thereafter, they would once again hit the road,
when the singing group known as the Shantells,

had finished performing their two shows before the event was done. When everyone appeared to be having fun.

The women of the female singing group would once again make their way out into the audience.

Where they would dance with some of the guys who were their secret admirers, or members of their fan base.

To fulfill the terms and conditions of their contract, that the services they render would be exact.

Suddenly, the DJ would soon announce that the song for the last dance was about to be played. As the night was coming to an end,

when the people had swung, rocked, and swayed to all the songs that the DJ had decided to spin. As the women from the Shantells singing group, would approach certain men.

In which they had a desire to dance with the chosen ones. As they would usually get their way, whether it be night, or whether it be day.

When Claresee had spotted a man in which she had chosen to solicit a dance, as she would make way and beseech him.

"A Kiss for the Last Dance!" She would say, when kissing the man gently on the jaw. Taking hold of his hand when leading him out onto the dance floor.

Where the people were dancing to the rhythm of a slow jam, slowly moving and spinning around, in tune with the slow jam's sound.

Dancing to the music of the last song. As it appeared that the song would drag on a little too long, when some of the quests had already gone.

As the women from the singing group known as the Shantells, would dance with the men as they carried on.

Pretending to be impressed, by some of the male quests, seeming to be fascinated by them. As they were only playing along, flirting with all the men exactly the same.

Tantalizing them as if it was just a game. Men who were believe to be their secret admirers, and others who were said to be their diehard fans.

However, when the gathering was over and done, Claresee, and the man in which she had danced, the last dance with.

He and she, just the two of them, had decided to stick together. As they ultimately wound up in one of the city's motel rooms, after spending a little time beneath the light of a full moon.

Then after an hour or two had gone by. Two gunshots were heard, as they rang out. Pow! Pow! When Claresee, one of the members of the Shantells singing group, was seen climbing out of a back window of the city's motel. Disappearing after engaging in a romantic affair, with the man who had fallen victim to her. As they were a pair.

When robbing him of a gold watch, swiping his hidden cash, from the inside of his automobile. Where the money was often stashed, as the man tried to keep it concealed.

She would quickly make way, leaving him behind lying in a pool of blood, soon after the gunshots were heard. When the crime had recently occurred.

Suddenly when the cops had arrived out at the motel, as they showed up on the scene. The woman was not around, she was nowhere to be found as it would seem.

However, after approximately two or three weeks had passed. When the Shantells singing group had finished with their previous engagement.

They would soon move on to another city, for their next appearance. During a time when it was scheduled to take place in just a matter of days.

Then as time rolled along. Late one night a man was seen running in the streets of the quiet city, when coming from the direction of a nearby lake.

Where he, and Claresee had been spending sometime together. Down by the lake inside the man's automobile,

where he was almost killed. When at close rang he had been shot in the head, and there he bled, but did not die.

Soon the cops were summoned. As they would speed straight out to the lake. In search of the person who had committed such coldhearted crime.

Which appeared to have been carried out exactly the same as the others, that had been occurring in the nearby cities, where men had been recently dying, when it was such a pity

Then as the cops had arrived, their searching eyes would noticed a woman swiftly moving into a mild breeze, amongst a span of tall trees, down by the lake.

Running wild, trying to get away, as they would give chase, hoping to get a glimpse of the woman's face as they raced.

Making their way on foot, following after the woman who was looking for a place to hide, as they drew near.

Thinking she was close by. When running in an eerie kind of atmosphere, near a graveyard where it has been said,

that ghosts rises up from the dead. Looking for someone who was still alive, that they may be embodied inside such person, as they were led.

That their souls may survive, in the wooded area where no man would dare to tread, as time was passing them by.

Soon the two cops would catch up with the fleeing female suspect, and based upon the blood found on her clothing, they would quickly place her under arrest.

Shoved her into the backseat of the policemen squad car, and transported her straight to the city jail, without fail.
Then after days had gone by, the cops would come up with the 22-caliber pistol, that had been found at the bottom of the nearby lake.

Which had been discovered by a homicide taskforce, when they were brought out, to drag the bottom of the muddy waters in search of the missing gun.

As they would eventually come up with the murder weapon, during a time when the trial was about to begin.

Wherefore the gun would be introduced into evidence, so that when during the trial. There would be no mistake, or any objections that the DA could not overcome.

Whenever the jury would begin to deliberate, that they may reach a just verdict. As everyone would certainly anticipate.

Soon after the testimony, and submission of the evidence were over and done. That the case may be won.

Eventually the woman would stand trial, for two of the four counts of homicide, and multiple counts into other crimes in which she had been accused of committing.

Whereas she was found guilty, on multiple counts of arm robbery, attempted murder, and for the killing of two of the four men, named in the homicide cases.

In various places, inside different cities. By a jury of seven men, and five women. Who would examine the evidence,

that the defense attorney could not defend, and what a back and forth trial it had been.
When the jury was quite willing to convict, after listening to the testimonies, and weighting the evidence. Against the person,

who would carryout such heinous crimes, with the gall to commit the evilness that fostered within their mind.

Whereby the woman would soon be given the mandatory sentence for a long prison stay, or sent way down yonder on death row, where the bad women go, for their crimes to pay.

When during the sentencing phase of the trial, at such time. The convicted member of the Shantells singing group, was standing quietly inside the courtroom.

Locked in shackles and chains, before the eyes and ears of those who had came, who were once her diehard fans.

Where she could have received the death penalty, thrust into the hot seat of the electric chair, under the DA's demands.

However, she was ordered to spend the rest of her life behind prison walls, inside old rusty bars, where the cells were quite small.

Beneath the watchful eyes of the armed guards, in a prison where times were hard. Where her fans,

could never again shake her hand. And from the cellblocks, and from the prison yard, she could never depart.

"A Kiss for the Last Dance"

Castle Of A Thousand Moons

It was during a time when the quiet shades of dawn had just began to disappear, when fading deep within the belly of the atmosphere.

Drifting out of the lingering darkness that fell from the night, giving rise to the early morning sunlight.

When the birth of the sunrise had began to bloom. As it would break across the city of Moapse quite soon

Whereby it would began shining throughout the awakening day, spreading its light every which way.

When soldiers from a neighboring city that was known as Chinchalk, had conquered the provenance of Moapse. In a land east of the Atlantic, where it was a whap.

When a war between the two regions had been ragging for more than two years. Whereas the city of Moapse had been battled and bruised, by the enemy who would stand accused.

When the soldiers of the advancing Chinchalk warriors had dethroned the king of Moapse, and beheaded him.

Soon the soldiers from the city of Chinchalk, would take the spoils and withdraw from the battled city of Moapse.

Leaving the war tore region behind, where quite a few men had been dying. Whereas some may have survived,

and lived to fight another day, perhaps if their king had stayed alive, as the life of him had been zapped.

When there was a woman whose name was Afielya Nightingale. Who was the queen of the city of Moapse,
as she was married to the king.

Who would answer to the name of King Jarrod, prior to him being captured, and eventually beheaded.

Wherefore the status of the woman was now, a queen without a king, when she would have to fulfill the duties of her deceased husband.

Until she could search out another husband that he may be king. Whereas it was a condition, that a queen be married to another member of the tribe.

Soon after a king dies, it was so required to take place in the city of Moapse, moments after a king's demise.

That the new husband may become king. To rule over the Moapse people, and be their guide, assuring them of his loyalty, if ever they were in doubt.

A ritual sort of thing that was to be swiftly carried out. It was so advised, as the people would be apprised.

Then as time moved on, Afielya, would rule over the city as best she could, waiting patiently for fate to intervene.

Send her another husband to replace the last king, who had fallen victim to the enemy, That he may reign over the people of Moapse, where Afielya would still be queen.
During this particular time she would have to tough it out, when trying to effectively find ways to rule over the people, as she searched about.

Looking for ways to rebuild the city which had been nearly destroyed. Something the Moapse people tried to avoid, but did not have adequate protection.

Attempting to create a plan to lead the people into a new direction, for sustaining a way of life where the people,

would be protected in case of another attack. That they may exist in a city where peaceful living was not a risk, and where the inhabitants would not get whacked.

Create a strategy to guard against, and prevent the blood thirsty Chinchalk warriors from returning to the scene.

That their intrusion be curtailed, and never again shall they have the strength to intervene, perpetrating their dirty tricks and deadly schemes.

Then as time dragged on, The queen had became discouraged, when she could not find another husband.

As she had searched the region over, including the closes cities and towns that spread near and around.

People within the city of Moapse complained, that nothing was being done to get them on the right path of living, that they may rebuild the war torn city.

Some of them would voice their opinions, for the need of another king, to lift them up out of the ashes of despair.
That the days of their lives may be spared, and the terrible destruction done to the war torn city may be repaired.

That their future emerge with a rebirth of the city, based upon a decree that had been declared, when certain women in the city of Moapse.

Would scorn, and tease the queen, when wearing black veils covering their faces, coming out of devilish places.

Complaining that Afielya, the queen, had eyes for their husbands, and that they did not trust her. Alluding to her as a queen without a king.

But be that as it may, as time pressed on. Afielya, would gather her entourage, and travel to a nearby city known as New Ropervill. In the company of her servants,

including her chamber maids. As they rode in chariots, and upon horseback, for more then three days.

When the path was narrow, and the journey was hard. Froth with perils in which they sought to avoid.

Carrying weapons of bows and arrows, machetes, and spears. To defend themselves in case of an attack.

Traveling for miles, to look further into the marrying matter that was required. Wherefore the queen had learned of a man, who went by the name of Tillay Munsue.

Wherefore many people would come from miles around, lured by a power that he claimed to be putting down, a power he claimed to possess, by anyone's guess.
Believed to have mystical powers that could mend a broken heart, and recall wasted dreams, which it seemed.

Turn your future around, give you the ability to have your hopes, and dreams revised on the flipside. Pursued and renewed, before the sun goes down.

Believed that he had the eyes of an eagle, and the vision of a prophet. To look into your world,

visualize a remedy of surprise. Which could set you free of your troubles, that your happiness would forever be.

The man she was referring to, was said to be a soothsayer, who sat on a throne inside the temple of wisdom.

Wherefore it was believed that he could instruct the queen, of traits in which she could utilize for finding a new husband, that he may be king.

Since the first husband had been beheaded by soldiers from the city of Chinchalk. Who had attack the city of Moapse, with such bloody and horrible mishaps.

Setting fires that burned high, as dark smoke would rise to the sky. Running people over with their horses when raging in the streets, as they suffered no defeat.

As the Chinchalk warriors had intruded upon the city to overthrow it, contribute to its downfall.

Whereby Afielya, was now known as the queen without a king. In which she had ultimately grown to be a shame, and appalled, grieving for the city's downfall.
As she would have to find a strong, and brave man to marry that he may become king. As it was required by a decree,

signed by all the king's men of what shall be, when a king's life comes to an end, and his spirit goes blowing in the winds.

Then during the time when she, and her entourage had arrived inside the city of New Ropervill, as they drifted in.

The people of New Ropervill would then give the queen a warm welcoming. As they had a feast, when they would dance, drink, eat, and be merry.

Where bare chest men, created bounding sounds of rhythm with their harps, and with the beating of their drums.

Spewing musical waves that could take hold of you.
In which they claimed that the sounds of the harps,

combined with the beating of the drums. Could entice the women, who were seen running around in the streets, half dressed more or less.

Watching you with their prying eyes, looking to get a view of your expressions. That they may enable themselves to communicate with your inner spirit.

Where a blueprint of your future may be laid out before the eyes of the soothsayer. Who claimed to maintain,

the ability to visualize the things in your future. As far as his eagle eyes claimed to see, what was likely to be.
A fantasy of long ago, still remains, simple and plain.
Of what would be lost, and what would be gain. as his world would keep spinning around.

Wherefore he was steeped in a world of the supernatural, where mystic wonders, have been said to abound.

Where friendly jaguars moved through the crowded streets of the city, as they were free to roam, whereas the streets were their home, in which they belonged.

Then as time progressed, the soothsayer, Tillay Munsue, would send for the queen to enter his temple of wisdom.

Then soon, she and her chamber maids were led by two of the temple guards, as they would reach the soothsayer's private chamber. As the queen,

was wearing a headdress adorned with blue diamonds, as golden stripes were intertwined, forming a unique design.

"Welcome, my honorable queen Afialya!" The soothsayer would say, as he would politely greet the queen.

When sitting on a bamboo throne, which was covered in zebra's skin. As he was getting cooled off with large feathery fans that provided a gust of wind.

As two of his female servants stood on each side of him, wearing short skirts made of straw. Gently moving the large feathery fans up and down without a flaw.

Circling them around. Spreading the cool air upon him as he sat on the throne, after the feast had wound down.
The queen would then bow before the soothsayer, with two of her chamber maids standing by her side. Carrying honey and incense to present to the host, as a surprise.

Soon she would began informing him, of the reason why, she had traveled so far to reach his city. Advising him that she had grown discouraged and weary.

Due to the fact that she had failed to find a brave man, to be king of the people, and for the people. And also to be her loving husband.

Since her first husband who was king, had been beheaded during an uprising between the two nations. The Moapse tribe, and the tribe of the Chinchalks.

Advising Tillay Munsue, the soothsayer, that she had came to seek his guidance. That he may assist her in finding a loving husband for herself,

and that the new husband may become the people king, and reign over them in the city of Moapse.

The soothsayer would call for the queen to come closer, and stand right before his eyes. When he advised her to extend her hands and arms, as he began to stroke her arms, and rub her palms. That he may feel a touch of her spirit. Claiming he could get an idea of why she was discouraged, and feeling weary.

Suddenly he would rise, and lift up the wooden staff that he held within his hand, pointing it toward the sky.

When he began chanting in a different tongue, whereas the queen could not understand the words that were being said. As she requested that the soothsayer speak in the tongue of her people instead.

However, she could feel the thrust of his imagination, in the thoughts of her anticipation. Then soon, he starting speaking in the dialect of the queen.

When he began to carryout a ritual, as the queen had agreed to take part in such event. Be hypnotized, in accordance to his request, by the powers he possessed.

Then when he had finished carrying out his ritual. He began to advise the queen, to build a castle upon a high hill, overlooking the city of Moapse.

Then after the castle would be completed, that she must claim the castle as her own. And the grounds in which it set upon shall be in honor of a new king.

That she must live there for the duration of a thousand moons. As the moon rise and fall for a thousand times.

And when during this particular period, she must not indulge romantically with any man, of any kind.

That only her chamber maids shall be permitted to enter the castle during such times. Which would be a sign of genuine things to come.

That the rise and fall of the moon a thousand times,

will serve as a purification period. That her heart and sold may be cleansed, and that she no longer be weary.

Whereby she may be a worthy bride, before all the people eyes, as the allotted cleansing time goes drifting by.

Informing the queen that the mystical period of the event, where the castle set high atop a hill overlooking the city.

And the rise and fall of the moon a thousand times. Will forever be known as the "Castle of a Thousand Moons."

Whereas the soothsayer began to cast small colorful bones before the eyes of the queen, putting her under a spell. Where she would be hypnotized, by the hands of the wise.

Until the day her wish would be propelled. Advising her to retain a number of swans to prance upon the royal grounds of the castle.

Where she must take daily walks among the flock of gorgeous birds, to sustain her gracefulness.

Wear rubies and sapphires to sustain a majestic beauty upon her face, for the pleasure of the future king's eyes. That her beauty may be realized.

As she would be compelled to carryout the soothsayer instructions all the way, through and through, each and everyday. In which she must rely.

Then as time moved along, the queen would travel back to the city of Moapse, along with her entourage.

As they would travel along a path, where large, man eating dragon lizards existed, within the belly of a muddy swamp.

Then suddenly as the travelers were moving past the muddy swamp. They were unaware of the dragon lizards,

that had took to the swamp in recent years, with no fear.
When the travelers would stop within a shady area near the mouth of the swamp.

To partake of refreshments, and relax for a quiet moment to ease their minds, and to give their horses a much needed rest at the same time.

When one of the packhorses began to act up. Bucking and jumping, with four hooves a stumping.

As the bucking animal could sense that the dragon lizards were near. Whereby the bucking horse's hind legs,

suddenly slipped down into the edge of the muddy swamp. Then swiftly! Three of the large dragon lizards rushed toward the struggling animal,

and savagely took hold of the horse's hind legs. Clamping down on them with their huge teeth and powerful jaws.

Dragging the animal deep into the muddy swamp. Where they mauled the beast and ripped the animal apart, right from the very start.

Quickly, Afielya, the queen, and her entourage would gather up their cargo and continue to move forward.
Making way back to the city of Moapse.

As she would cling to the instruction that were given her by the soothsayer. During his ritual as she was hypnotized.
Whereby she would carry them out as it was required, have the builders to erect the castle exactly as planed.

Where atop the nearest tallest hill, the castle must appear. Existing and overlooking the city, and there it shall stand.

Strong and tall on a hill, above a bed of sand within the regional hemisphere, that glitters from the rays of the sunlight, and from the light of a starry night.

Then on certain clear and bright nights, only the queen eyes, could see silhouettes of the castle, shining within the face of the silvery moon.

By the spell of her hypnotized eyes. When wishing that her wedding day would be coming real soon.

As the moon would spread its gentle light, upon her face, as she watched from the windows of the royal place.

Peeping down below, and gazing up at the face of the moon when it began to glow.

Then after nearly three years had went by. Afielya, the queen, had carried out all the soothsayer's instructions in the exact order, in which they were given to her.

And when time had pressed on, the mystical feat was complete, and the undertaking of the queen's task had been accomplished.

Wherefore the hypnosis that was put upon her, had been lifted. Then when the early morning would blossom into the atmosphere, the man of her heart desire would appear,
as if out of the clear blue sky. Standing in the way of the sun, during an early morning sunrise.

Wherefore the two of them would immediate fall in love, as she ran to meet him. When the queen's happiness would suddenly, reconvene.

Soon they would have a royal wedding, as the two of them were married. With swans, flamingos, and peacocks.

Strutting around within the grounds of the castle. Showcasing their elegance and beauty, for a graceful display.

Emphasizing the royalty of their wedding day, that gave royal status only to the groom, and to the bride.

Children were given leave to take rides on Shetland ponies, as the guests would be entertained, having a party within the rose garden, as they all came.

Where women with the voices of an angel would sing, as golden wedding bells would magically rang.

Where the moon would rise at twilight, and began dancing across the mystic sky, deep into their wedding night.

Then at last, real soon. When the wedding was all over and done, under the sun. The groom would become king, and the bride, would be his queen.

"Castle of a Thousand Moons"

Blue Diamonds
Of Twilight

Behold the colorful bluish stars that blooms sometime during dusk, to which only a few eyes have ever seen.

The evening stars that rarely beams, quit evasive, and perhaps never seen by any of us, of unfamiliar faces.

When shining only after the last flaming segment of the sun has burned, when the evening is done.

And disappears during the last phase of the evening atmosphere, as the sky reveals.

Which hangs above a warm and dense climate, amid an isolated segment of the southern hemisphere before the coming of night.

Which are referred to by those who lives in the land, as the "Blue Diamonds of Twilight."

That comes in view as the autumn leaves begins to fall from the overloaded branches,

that bears a cluster of flowers as they hang from the resting trees, which spouts about within the summer breeze. Following the last,

of the summertime sunshine, that burns out at the ends of the seasons as it unwinds.
When the warm summer evenings begins to slowly drift away, twisting and turning through the ends of day.

Painting the atmosphere with a touch of reality, that your heart can feel, as it appears.

To hold back the darkness of night, that awaits beyond the distant sky for awhile.

Making way for the "Blue Diamonds of Twilight." That sparkles as with jewels from the night,

taken from the lighter shades of darkness, before the night is in full bloom.

When blending with a hint of day light, and a hint of darkness, none to soon.

Taken out of a deep dark pit, before the stars of night are lit, and before the rising of the blue moon begins to bloom.

Which soothes the eyes of your insight. When the evening begins to silently unravel whenever the time is right.

Before the "Blue Diamonds of Twilight," allows for the blue moon to awaken,

and kisses the powdery face of darkness. Reflecting the luster of pearly light, when silently rising before your eyes.
As the sunset burst into a display of glamour, and began to spread, turning the sky fiery red.

As the shades of twilight hangs in wait,
only for a moment in time, that lies straight ahead as it begins to thrive,

as if hanging by a thread. Painting a picture of grace and beauty, for your eyes only.

Creating a scenery of poetry between the light of day, and the shades of night.

Prior to the awakening of the sleeping stars, as they too, begins glistening as blue diamonds in the sky.

As if stones of precious jewels, flickering across the heights, far and wide, when lighting up the piers of the hemisphere.

Soon after the "Blue Diamonds of Twilight," have paved the way for the coming of such a romantic night.

When dreams of your sweetheart begins to blossom within the windows of your mind, of a love so fine.

During such moments that turns the pages of time. As the sun races beneath the horizon,

when the night owls raises up and takes flight,
before the shades of twilight have gone,
and swiftly disappears from the atmosphere, when only meant to be short lived.

Dispersing the feeling and desire for you to roam, as the shades of twilight is not meant to last very long.

When the stargazers gather beneath the starry light, in search of a bright and romantic night.

When the hidden wonder of a soft summer evening, gives way to the "Blue Diamonds of Twilight," as the occurrence ignites, and gives birth to the stars of pearly light.

Following the fading of the afternoon, when the day is consumed. Which gives way to the rising of the blue moon,

when it begins to shine in the night, crystal bright, as it begins to bloom, quite soon.

"Blue Diamonds of Twilight"

A Date For The Wolf Man

The sky was cold of winter, on a late foggy evening when it was rather dark and dreary. As if the jaws of the black night, had reached out, and swallowed up the fading sun.

When you could hear the gusting winds whistling through the trees, tearing away at the dying winter leaves.

As a mist began to hang in the air prior to first night, when falling rather light. Whereas your eyes could plainly see.

A strange looking ship plying forward against the wind, coming out of the roaring sea slowly moving in.

As it began lowing its sails, and dropping anchor within the waters near the city known as, Two Crow. Where many ships would come and go.

When a man born as James Crawford, had made his way back to the seaside mountain town. Where the mountains setback and rises high, nearly touching the sky.

As he would disembark from the incoming ship. Making his way back to the rural part of the city, where he and his deceased parents once lived.

Deep inside the back woods, where he used to laugh and play, runner around with the wolves when he was just a boy, bursting with curiosity in everyway.

Somehow figuring that he was part wolf, preferring to spend time with the beasts instead of playing with his toys.

A few years ago he had been fired upon, by over zealot police officers, as they were trying to shoot him down.

When he stood high atop the Two Crow Bridge, in a quest to escape the barrage of gunfire that was coming in his direction, when he had no protection.

Trying to scamper away, as the cops began blasting at him, destine to take him out, without a doubt. Then in regards to the rule of law, it was neglected, and redirected.

Whereby James would plunge deep into the scarlet lake, splashing down in the cold waters that flowed below, scrambling for a safe place to go.

And when the cops searched the waters for James, thinking that he may have been shot, he could not be found in spite of him going down.

Some folks believed that James might have drown, others claimed he could have pulled up stakes, and left the mountain town.

Whereas in the city of Two Crow, before he grew up and went away. Some of the boys at the high school in which he attended, began calling him the Wolf Man.

Due to the fact that he had grew up with the wolves, playing and eating with them. During a time when his father was nurturing and caring for the animals.

Kept them inside a large pen, where he would feed and study the beasts, had been experimenting with the wolves, since the very first day that the venture began.
As he and his wife raised their son along with the wolves, until their lives came to an end. During the time when James was a little boy, till he grew into his teen years.

His father used to feed the wolves special meals, which was part of an experiment to enhance their ability to survive in the wild, and help them grow big and strong.

He would then release them permanently back into the wild that they may survive on their own, seize a viable territory within the wilderness, to have as their home.

Then during the meantime, James would get a hold of some of the red meat, and other types of food laced with chemical substances when it was fed to the wolves.

Then as time went by, during James teenage years, he began to take on some of the features of the wolves. Perhaps as a result of eating some of their food.

Whereby prior to him finishing high school, his ears had grew to be slightly pointed, like that of a wolf.

And his facial features were similar to those of a wolf,
it would certainly appear, something that could not be concealed.

Also at night, his eyes would glow from the rays of the moonlight. As his upper body would slightly lean forward when walking upright.

And as time moved on, he began weaving some of the wolves pelts into clothes. Wearing the warm animal's fur, whenever the weather was cold.
When at various times he would become aggressive and quite bold. Whereby some of the boys who knew him, and went to the same high school as he.

Were the first to began calling him the Wolf Man, said he was cool, defiant of all the rules, whenever he choose.

Whereas when he was a boy, the wolves accepted him as one of their own, and wherever they would roam, James would often tag along.

As he would somehow grow up thinking that he was part wolf. Some folk claimed he was rather strange, prone to do bad things, stating that perhaps the boy had gone insane.

When he had grew up with the wolves. Following the time when his father decided to move out into the wooded area of the city.

Along with his wife, and their son, James. When he was a small child, during the time when his father would study the wolves, observing the manner in which they behaved, as they hunted and played.

However, after approximately seven years had past, James had now returned to the city of Two Crow,

for the vary first time since that day, when he decided to slip away. Once again making his home deep inside the back woods upon his return.

As he began squatting in the same location, where his family lived when he was just a boy, where he would watch the rising of the morning sun until it was done.
He had survived, and stayed alive after the cops tried to take him out. Shooting at him when he stood high atop the Two Crow Bridge, approximately seven years before.

During such time when a mob of men went in search of him. Hunting inside a cave, thought to be his secret hiding place, prior to them shooting at the Wolf Man.

When the gun toting men gave chase, as they were carrying fiery torches, looking for ways to take him out.

When the burning flames gave them a path of light, as they went searching deep into the darkness of night.

Whereby you could hear the barking of bloodhounds, the dogs that would race across the hunting grounds with saliva dripping from their mouths.

They were leading the mob through the wilderness, and through the open fields looking for blood to spill.

When the Wolf Man had been falsely accused of bloody murder, of a woman who was once his companion.

Whereas there was no reason for him to do so, in the wake of their mutual understanding. When between the two of them only friendly vibes would flow.

Now that he had returned to the city, things had changed in the town of Two Crow, and to him it seemed quite strange.

When only a hand full of folks still remembered his name. Since the time when he was only a little boy, as he took roots within the city to grow.
His mother and father had been killed in a plane crash, an accident where others had also perished long ago.

Whereby no one aboard the aircraft would survive, before the Wolf Man had gone away on that rather bizarre day.

After being shot at by the cops when he plunged deep into the waters down below, and disappeared. Escaping a barrage of hot lead, that was whizzing right past his head.

Upon his return he would move back into the rundown shack of a log cabin, where he and his parents used to live.

As he would take up with the business of the wolves, where his father left off. When he began raising and studying the beasts, helping them to survive in the wild.

Then as time went by the Wolf Man began to get lonely. Whereby he wanted to be with a woman, to fulfill the emptiness that fostered within his heart.

Howling in the night, beneath the pale moonlight. As the empty space within his heart, seem to be tearing him apart.

Then at certain times he would go out, and climb atop one of the tallest buildings that stood within the city.

When howling at the moon, to suppress the pain that his heart would feel, when he knew of no love to be real.

Found time to leisurely take walks through the marketplace, during certain periods when the atmosphere seemed to be laced, with a scent reminding him of his childhood days.
He would also leisurely stroll through the cobblestone streets of the city, during the times when it was said by the inhabitances, that the moon runs with blood on certain mystic night.

It has been said that the moon bled whenever it would begin to glow, turning blood red right before your eyes.

Where street dancers would emerge with black masks covering their faces, as they would dance to a tropical beat, for silver coins and dollar bills.

To be tossed into a basket that set before their eyes, that they may be paid, as onlookers went passing by.

As the Wolf Man would be wearing a long link, dark grayest coat, made from the wolves fur during the winter cold. Woven into a style to protect him from the elements when the four winds blows.

With a hood attached, that partially covered his face and head. Searching for someone to accept him regardless of his appearance whoever they were, hoping for it to occur.

He would soon overhear a conversation, when someone would mention, that there was a dating service that had came to town. Known as the Love Connection.

Where the owner of the place could get you a date. Hook you up with the person who may have been born to be your mate, for the fee of a very small rate.

Wolf Man would then make a telephone call, and ask to speak to someone who could assist him in his endeavor.

"Hello! This is the Love Connection," said the woman who took the call. "May I help you please?" she inquired.

"Yeah," said the Wolf Man. "My name is James Crawford, and I'm looking for a lady to which I can spend sometime with, have a little fun, one-on-one."

"James Crawford, who attended Two Crow high school?" The woman asked. "Yeah, that's me," he replied.

Then the woman would let go a loud scream, uh-uh uh-uh!!!!!!!!!, Wolf Man, is that you! Are you back in town again, how have you been?" she would ask.

"This is Larjean Conwell, do you remember me?" She inquire. "Yeah! I remember you, for sure," he replied, when seeming to be quite surprised.

"A Date for the Wolf Man!" The woman would shout out, as she began to collect his information, and feed it into the computer data base.

Soon the dating service would match the Wolf Man up with a woman, who went by the name of Fast Fanny.

She had been living fast and loose for quite sometime, had the thought of good loving running through her mind.

Whereby she was now searching for that special someone, to spend the rest of her life with. Since she was now well into the stage, of an advanced marrying age.

Looking to get away from that no count, live-in boyfriend of hers. Who had been misusing and abusing her,
the whole time they were together, as if he was a mad man.
Finally she wanted to get away from him for good, as fast as she could. Settle down with someone else,

find a little place outside of town. Where she could easily live, in harmony with another, who may have lots of love to give.

It had been arranged, for Fast Fanny to meet up with James, the person who was known as the Wolf Man. Inside a nearby coffee shop.

Then as she arrived, she went inside, stood within the doorway. Wearing a lovely dress with matching high heels, in an attempt to look her very best.

As she was filled with a certain amount of cheer. Reached up and removed the dark glasses from her eyes.

When she began to take a glancing look around inside the place, with a smile upon her face, as she continued to gaze.

Then she would commence sashaying toward the back of the coffee shop, where she began to quietly callout to her computer date in a whispering voice.

"James, James, James!" She softly said, as she was moving towards the back of the designated meeting place.

Then suddenly, James stepped out from a back section of the building, when emerging out of the dark shadows, as he laid eyes on Fast Fanny. "A Date for the Wolf Man?" he would quietly asked, when he approached the woman.

Then as she caught a glimpse of him, she began to shake with fear, as he appeared before her eyes with a facial profile, and a body slightly resembling that of a wolf.

Quickly she turned, and began to run away, bursting back out of the front door of the place, when he gave chase calling out to her.

"Wait! Wait! Don't run, wait just one minute! My name is James, and you are my date," he would shout out and say.

Then there! Right then and there! Just up ahead, as Fast Fanny had ran past a crowd, screaming aloud.

There stood the woman's no count, live-in boyfriend. As she unknowingly ran straight toward him,

bumping right into the mad man. As he began fussing and cursing at her, blurting out his demands.

"Where have you been my woman? I have been looking hell over high waters for you," he yelled.

Then he began beating upon her, slapping her around, knocking her down to the ground. "Don't you ever leave me again!" He shouted.

Suddenly the Wolf Man came upon the scene. "Stop hitting the woman," he would say to the no count boyfriend, in a heavily toned of voice.

Then quickly, the no count boyfriend came at the Wolf Man, with a large tree branch in hand, trying to club the Wolf Man upside the head.

When Wolf Man grabbed hold of him, and slammed the fellow hard to the ground. Striking him with several hard blows.

The Wolf Man would then kindly reach down, and pick the woman up, when she was obliged, gave him a smile.

Suddenly a gunshot rang out. Pow! As the boyfriend was aiming a forty-four magnum at the Wolf Man,

but wound up putting a bullet in the woman's back, to be exact. There she lay dead, as her body fell to the ground.

When she made not another sound, as blood oozed out of her back, and dripped from her head.

Then there, the Wolf Man grabbed hold of the woman's boyfriend, as they struggled over the gun, when suddenly.

The Wolf Man snapped the boyfriend's neck, when you could hear the sound of the man's neck as it cracked. When he would fall to the ground lying flat on his back.

As the man would quickly die, with blood oozing from the corners of his eyes. Wherefore the Wolf Man would cradle the woman's body within his large muscular arms.

When you could see him moving beneath the pale moonlight, carrying her back to the place of the dating service in the dead of night.

Where he would gently lay the woman's body down near the front entrance of the place, when in deep silence. As he would walk away without words to say.
Then as minutes turned into hours the cops had discovered that the Wolf Man was back in town, and that he was not dead as it had been said, as word would float around.

Some believed that he had been shot down, by policemen gun rounds, or drowned a few years ago. But really, no one would ever know, during such time before.

After the cops had fired their weapons at him, during that day when he stood atop the Two Crow Bridge long ago.

Then plunged into the scarlet lake after being shot at, as he would disappear and could not be found. It was now realized that he had left town.

The cops would soon begin searching for the Wolf Man the second time around, throughout the city, with no pity.

When at this particular time they were going to charge him for the murder of the woman. Who went by the name of Fast Fanny, whose blood had been spilled, when she was shot and killed.

Charge him for the killing of the woman's boyfriend, who were found lying dead near the coffee shop outside of town, a few hours after the sun had gone down.

One of the cops had a vendetta against the Wolf Man, since the earlier days. As he was raving about how the Wolf Man had long ago, violated his woman.

Climbed into an open window when his heart was filled with lust, forced himself to engage in stolen romance with the woman, as he thought he must.
She was a woman who went by the name of Ulissy, and the officer who made the claim was one of the cops.

Who had taken shots at the Wolf Man, before he left town, when they were trying to shoot him down.

During the time when Wolf Man stood atop the Two Crow Bridge, that stretched across scarlet lake. When he plunged into the cold waters down below and could not be found.

The officer who harbored the vendetta against the Wolf Man, claimed that when they find his whereabouts.

That he was going to send the beast swimming down to the bottom of the sea. Only this time around he won't be coming back, for a matter of fact.

Some folks claimed that the woman, in which the officer was referring to, was nothing but a Jezebel. Who had caused lots of trouble,

spreading lies and falsifying alibis. A woman who appeared to have came straight up from the bottom of hell.

And what she said about the Wolf Man, did not have the rang of truth, but would bring on trouble just as well.

Whereby the Wolf Man early years, appeared to have woven his destiny. In the direction of chaos, when he would feel a need to flee.

Since the times when he was falsely accused of committing criminal acts, that would not let him be, so plain to see.
Then as time would progress, Wolf Man would once again telephone the dating service, to search for another woman, to which he could spend sometime with.

When he would once again speak to the woman named Larjean Conwell. In which the both of them had attended the same high school, during days gone by.

And when the phone had rung, Larjean would pickup. "Hello, this is the Love Connection dating service, may I help you?" The woman would ask.

The Wolf Man would then request another date. In search of a woman to spend sometime with, to ease his loneliness, and the burden of his heartache.

Wherefore he and his date, could find a way to spend sometime where lovers play. If she would, and if she may.

As he continued to stay, way out yonder in that old rundown shack, in a wooded area of the city where he grew up as a boy.

As he carried on his father's legacy, raising a bunch of wolves, and experimenting with the beasts as his father had done. Which was once his father's main concern.

"Well, hi there James! This is Larjean of the Love Connection dating service. How are you doing once again?" She asked.

"Doing good," said the Wolf Man. "Looking for a woman to spend sometime with. Do you have such a person that can appease my desires, put a few sparkles in my eyes?"

"But James, what happened to the last date we arranged for you, did anything go wrong?" the dating service agent would inquire.

"Just a lonely waste of time," said the Wolf Man. "What can you do for me this time around?" He asked.

Little did anyone know that the cops had bugged the dating service telephones, planted their listening devices inside, where nothing could be denied.

"A Date for the Wolf Man," said Larjean, the dating agent. "Well James, I will be most happy to be your date,

and go out with you to spend sometime. Where we can found a place to have a picnic, and there we can unwind."

When the two of them got together, they made their way out to the river on the other side of town, miles away from the Two Crow Bridge.

Where they were beginning their picnic, as the evening sun was beaming down through the surrounding trees, brushing across a canopy of falling leaves. Near a hillside road, where the four-leaf clovers spins and grows.

Then suddenly, the cops arrived. Speeding into the area as they swerved their vehicle near the place where the couple were sitting, to arrest the Wolf Man, or shoot him down.

Suddenly they would exit their vehicle with guns at their disposal. "Hold it right there Wolf Man! And put your hands up!" The cops yelled.
"You are under arrest!" they would shout out. When suddenly, they began blasting at the Wolf Man with their weapons, trying to shoot the Wolf Man down.

As the gunshots would rang out making noisy sounds, could be heard from miles around. Pow! Pow! Pow!!!!!!
When gun smoke billowed high into the sky.

As the woman was yelling and screaming at the cops.

"Don't shoot the Wolf Man! Let him be! Let him be!" You could hear her calling out, but the cops refused to stop.

Then there! The Wolf Man was hit, by a piercing slug in the upper part of his body that came from a barrage of gunfire, as he quickly scampered away, and dove into the nearby river with no delay.

Leaving behind blood stains upon the sandy banks of the waters, as he fled and profusely bled.

Wherefore it would be the second time within seven years, that the Wolf Man had been setup to be killed. When no one knew whether he was still alive, or whether he died.

Some folks claimed that he was still alive, even after being shot by the cops, they believed somehow he still remains.

Some contends that he may have swam away, leaving his footprints in the sand as he stray into another day, and managed to survive.

"A Date for the Wolf Man"

SWEET MONEY

The day had almost pass by on a late Saturday evening, when a man named Blue Ray Humfrey, had just walked out onto the streets of Lake Providence.

When emerging out of a gambling hall, a place where he frequented when indulging in games of chance. Then after he had finished playing his favorite games.

Most of the times he would walk outside with his winnings in hand, counting it for accuracy, which was his main concern when the gambling was done.

Then when he was sure of the amount of cash he had won. He would then raise it up to his mouth, where he would suddenly kiss it, "Sweet Money!" he would say.

When turning his head roundabout from side-to-side, to see if anyone was coming his way, peeping from the corners of his eyes, Making sure no one was standing close by. harboring intentions to keep them at bay.

Then he would quickly, shove the cash deep down inside a front pocket of his pants, as he walked away from the place, with a smile upon his face.

People who knew him were aware of the habit in which he had developed, always thinking that it was rather funny.

Where unto most of the folks that socialized with him, he became known as "Sweet Money."

During the progression of time, it appeared that he had a knack for winning at any type of gambling game. Whether he was slick and sly, or just a lucky kind of guy.

Gained a little notoriety and fame, down Louisiana's way. As a man who knew how to predict the outcome of any type of game, claiming that Lady Luck knew his name.

Perhaps it could be, that he would use slight of hand, which no one could understand, how he would always manipulate a game of chance.

And for this specific reason some of the single ladies around town would began gravitating to him, to spend sometime, with money on their minds.

At various times you could see him walking the streets with perhaps two, or three lovely ladies hanging onto his arms.

Most often when he was dress up in a three piece suit, with colors from the rainbow. Some being red, others being green at certain times. Some being purple, when others were blue of a different kind.

When wearing different styles of velvet hats, that would blend in with the shade of his fancy outfits, with a style of his own in which he would commit.

Especially when the streetlights were well lit, As he would come up with ways to make profitable bets, with the kind of luck that brings on big bucks.

Fraternizing with ladies of the night. Believing that they would treat him right. Said they were lovely and out of sight.
The ones with whom he would hang around, soon after the son goes down. When making his daily bets during a time before the sunset.

Where unto his eyes they would appear to blossom, into princessed and queens. The loveliest gals his eyes had ever seen, as they were drawn to certain men of wealthy means.

Whereas he would wine and dine some of the ladies, with the money he would so often win, time-and-time again.

When he would take them to fancy restaurant, and swinging nightclubs. Women who would help him relax by giving him a massage, or perhaps an invigorating back rub.

"Sweet Money," you are so kind to me, so wonderful and nice," one of the females would say to him when intending to be precise.

As women were enchanted by his slick style, generosity, and his alluring charm, as they would cling to his arms.

Nonetheless, he was not a happy man. Despite knowing how to play the winning hand, knew how to call up Lady Luck,

to bring in the big bucks. When winning at almost any type of game, feeling the urge to take a chance.

But be that as it may, he did not have that special someone in which he would often dream, to be a part of his life.

The dream lady in which he would sometime envision to be his wife. She who could inspire, and fulfill the desirer of his heart, in ways that they may never drift apart.

Then as weeks turned into months, he began to play the lottery. When he would pick the lucky numbers and win big.
Spin the lucky wheel that would give him a thrill.

As he began dancing across the gambling hall floor, when doing one of his familiar jigs. Rocking and rolling, happy as can be, singing like a lark perched high up in a tree.

Whereas things were happening so fast for him, as if he had been thrust into a daze, at least in a couple of ways. Thinking that he was the hottest guy in town.

When soon! The good, the bad, and the ugly would began to hang around. Searching for a chance to get a piece of him,

whether to build him up, or to tear him down. Use him to boost up their lifestyles that their wealth may abound.

Then suddenly, on one fine Saturday night. When Blue Ray Humfrey had stepped outside from one of the gambling halls, after winning big and standing tall.

When he would began to count his winnings as always. Wearing one of his colorful three piece suits, along with a matching velvet hat with a smile upon his face.

Then suddenly, there came a woman out of the dark shadows, who had him zeroed within the scope of her eyes. Zoomed him right smack-dab into her sights, on one such cool and
mystical night.

With prying eyes, donned in a bright red dress, ready to be his catch. To be taken as his winning prize, as she would certain try with a winning smile.
When she would sashay toward him, quietly coming up from behind, when tapping him on one of his shoulders in just a matter of time.

As he would then quickly spin around. "Hey! 'Sweet Money," the woman would softly speak. As she looked into his eyes,

when he would perceive her as such a pleasant surprise, brought out the shine in his great big smile.

"Well hello there my little angel, what might your name be?" the man would ask. As he removed his velvet hat, from the crown of his head.

gently nodding before the woman to show her respect. Thinking that she might just be one of his lucky bet, the kind that brings no regret.

However, before he may once again, have a chance to spin the winning wheel around, for him, the sun may have already gone down.

"My name is Waylean," the woman replied, as she was blinking her eyes and showing him a lovely smile.

Flirting with him as with a sense of joy, to build up an attraction that may take place between any girl and boy.

He would soon take the woman into a restaurant and buy her a gourmet dinner, complete with champagne. Took her to a picture show that they may be entertained.

Then as time moved along, he had fell hard for her, said she was the queen of his dreams. Felt as though he was swimming in a sea of love,

hypnotized and floating amongst the brightest stars above. Asked her to be his wife, believing that she was awfully nice, sweeter then sugar and spice.

But what he failed to realize, was that she was out for show, running a game on him more than he would ever know.

Since she was already married to another. Playing him for a fool, in opposition to the lovers golden rules

Hiding the fact that she was already married to a man named Limptoe Bradly, Keeping her marriage to him as a hidden secret. When they were both living together in his mother's house sleeping on a couch.

Which began after his mother had passed away perhaps a year ago or so, to this day. Whereas the house had now gone into foreclosure.

When the two of them, Waylean, and Limptoe, her first husband. Would have to vacate the premises and find another place of their own, if they were to have a home.

Wherefore Limptoe had concocted a scheme. When he was aware that "Sweet Money" had purchased a brand new house, as it would seem.

Along with a fleet of new automobiles, in which Waylean would get behind each wheel. A large bank account that he had accidentally revealed.

When Limptoe, the first husband began to set the scheme in motion, along with Waylean. Advising her to change her name, even though she would still be one in the same.

Advising her to go, and get married to "Sweet Money," who had proposed to her. Then run a game on him, a love game in which he could not win. Figure out a way that his luck may come to an end.

By tantalizing him, conjuring up a wonder within his mind by showing him a goodtime. Get him thinking that they were deeply in love, as two romantic doves.

By being awfully nice, pretending that she wanted to be his wife, with kisses as sweet as honey. To blind the eyes, of the man who went by the name of "Sweet Money."

Then as time moved on, she would meet up with him, and accept his marriage proposal, and be his wife.

As Limptoe insisted, even though she would be taking on the role of a bigamy. A person involved in more than one marriage.

As she would now be married twice. Wherefore her first husband was the man she was now living with, whose name was Limptoe.

Whereas this time around she was about to get married to "Sweet Money," and be his wife as well, with plans to hear the sounds of more wedding bells.

Be married to a couple of guys at the same time, two separate matrimony that would somehow intertwine. Putting things in a bind, enough to blow any man's mind.

Then as time moved forward, "Sweet Money," and Waylean were married. When wedding bells would rang, and humming birds would sing.

Then! Soon thereafter, when the wedding was over and done. "Sweet Money" would throw a big shindig,

where folks would drink champagne, dance to happy music when engaging in lots of fun things.

During a time when he was passing out hundred dollar bills, exposing his wealth, something he could not conceal.

Then at that exact time, there stood her first husband, Limptoe. Standing watch in the shadows when left behind.

As Waylean would go away on her second honeymoon, to a secluded oasis a few mile outside of town, after being recently married to "Sweet Money," pretending to settle down.

Then during the honeymoon there stood Limptoe, the first husband, lurking close by watching from the outside.

Observing what the two newlywed were doing to each other, on their honeymoon stay, the very first day.

But it did not bother him, not one little bit, did not matter. Nothing disturbing would creep cross his mind. He was all about getting the money, didn't really care about the honey.

Then after the fiery scheme of Waylean second wedding had burned out, and the honeymoon had came to an abrupt end, Waylean would often go shopping.

And as for her love, "Sweet Money" had became obsessed, when he would give her anything, whereas she was the type of female who wanted the very best, and nothing less.

But it made no difference to him, as he craved the sweet taste of her love, and had to have it at any cost, or his heart would be lost.

Then during such times when she claimed to be gone shopping. On the contrary she would go and spend time with her first husband, Limptoe.

Way out yonder where the whirlwinds blow, in the wide open countryside, where she and her first husband would abide.

When he would advise her that it was about time, to get the ball rolling. Time for he and she, to begin spending the money in which they were entitled.

Stating that he was tire of living in the old shack where his mother used to live. When Waylean was living large, staying with her second husband, and driving new cars

As the first husband, Limptoe, was now insisting that it was about time, for the both of them to go and takeover the second husband's brand new house.

That they may have a new home of their own. By getting rid of "Sweet Money," carryout their plan, in which the both of them were sure to understand.

Then as hours faded into days. Waylean would lure her second husband out to the countryside, to the home in which she was claiming as her own, promising him a goodtime.

Assuring him that they would certainly be alone, just he and she. With words that were filled with deceit, that played upon the rhythm of his heartbeat, but the sound of them were soft and sweet.

In which he was being taken for a ride, but the love he possessed for her, had blinded the wisdom of his eyes. When he was to blind to see, a picture of true love, and the way it supposed to be.

Where unto him, her love was as a tasty treat, and his heart and soul, was hook on a kind of love that he could not defeat.

Then when they arrived out to the place, she invited him inside. "Come on in 'Sweet Money' my dear love," she would say as the two newlyweds would make their way.

Where he began to tell her, about the plans he had came up with, to fix up her place, and make it very nice, since she was now his wife.

As she was all smiles, looking at him through those big and beautiful deceitful eyes. "OK my darling," she would reply.

"Sweet Money,' you are so nice to me, and I am so happy to be your wife," she would say, as she gave him a smile when blinking her sparkling eyes as they made way.

When kissing him on the cheek, in a quest to show him the kind of love in which he was destine to seek.

Then during this particular time, Limptoe, the first husband, was waiting outside. Sneaking around by the windowpanes when he began to spy, standing nearby as he came.

Watching the interactions of the love affair that Waylean, and her second husband was going through, as they were carrying on before long.

However it did not mean nothing to Limptoe, even though by law, Waylean was his lawfully wedded wife, but his heart was as cold as ice. Whereby he had encouraged Waylean to be married twice.

Suddenly when the romance was about to come to an end, that had taken place between she and her second husband. When the night was late, and time was swiftly moving towards daybreak.

She would then bring out two cold classes of champagne, in which she had spiked, with a substance designed to knock the man out, sometime after midnight.

In an attempt to take her second husband's life. That she and her first husband, Limptoe, would receive all the possessions that belong to her second husband, Blue Ray Humfrey, better known as "Sweet Money."

Then! When "Sweet Money," would take a few gulps of the spiked champagne, he would soon collapse to the floor,
but did not die.

When having trouble breathing, and a problem with his eyes. When Waylean would suddenly call out to the first husband, Limptoe. Who was outside the door with groves on his hands.

When he would soon stroll into the house as he was standing close by. Where he would grab hold of a sharp knife to finish the man off, carryout their plan.
As he kneeled down next to the man, then with a quick swipe of the knife, he slit the man's throat, from side-to-side, and there the man would soon die.

They would then drag his body outside into the backyard of the foreclosed house, and dig a shallow grave.

Where they would bury the man, and there he lay, just before the break of day when no one was watching.

Consequently a few people in Lake Providence would report "Sweet Money" as missing. Stating that they had seen Waylean and her first husband, Limptoe,

spending time in Sweet Money's brand new house. When she had told the FBI that her second husband, Blue Ray Humfrey, had gone out of town for the weekend.

Stating that only a few days it had been, but to her surprise he had not yet returned, not even before the rising of the morning sun.

Then when the FBI would soon get wind of a report suggesting foul play. When they would launch an investigation,

into the disappearance of the man named Blue Ray Humfrey, better known as "Sweet Money." When the nights were mellow and the days were sunny.

The FBI would eventually make their way out to the countryside, where they would soon arrive out at the vacant house. Where Waylean and Limptoe had recently been staying.

When the police officers would bring in bloodhounds, and comb the area for any kind of clue, or evidence to be found.

As they would soon discover a shallow grave in the backyard of the foreclosed house, in a matter of days since the murder had taken place.

Then as the news of the man's disappearance would spread throughout the region, the FBI would receive information that a man named Limptoe was attempting to flee the city.

When a high speed chase would ensue, as Limptoe was trying to go on the run. However, the high speed chase would soon be over and done, when he was arrested on suspicion of murder.

And when Waylean was brought in for questioning, she would also be arrested in connection to the crime. Then by the two of them, the commission of the crime had been combined.

Whereas both of them were found to be involved, when carrying out their deadly scheme, as proof of the crime would evolve.

Then when the saga of the case had played out, the convicted felons were thrust into the darkness of a penitentiary, where their days would no longer be sunny.

Where they would be spending lots of hard luck time. Inside the pen. Where by none of the player would ever win again.

"Sweet Money"

Just A Touch Of Your Love

"Just a Touch of Your Love," is what I lone to embrace.
To enhance my cloudy days, as they go dragging by,
slowly before my eyes.

When wishing, and hoping that you were still here,
snuggled right up by my side, in the heat of the moment.

Where my eyes can gaze upon your lovely face, as only
a small portion of your love still persist.

Left over from the true love we once knew, where only
a touch of it continue to exist.

As I spent precious moments with you. When in the
beginning, your love found its way deep down inside
the pit of my heart.

Which led to sweet romance, that thrust me into a
trance prior to us growing apart.

As it took a strong compassionate hold of me, right
from the start. When it blossomed, and finally grew,
splashed by the morning's dew.

Whereby only a small pebble of it still remains, and
lingers on, as most of it has been washed away by the
pouring rain.

That once crept into our lives eventually, when
something went awfully wrong, before long.

Then our love affair would never be the same, a relationship that was in doubt, and played out, when it would soon refrain.

A love that once blossomed with the wings of spring, and with warmth from the morning sunshine, before the fullness of a day could unwind.

Whereas every once in awhile, a small piece of it takes to the sky. Blowing in the wind, then finds its way back into my heart once again.

From whence my emotions derives, as the mood of me becomes energized, feeling as though I can fly. As my world once again seems to burst alive.

Wherefore with "Just a Touch of Your Love,"
I get a glowing sense of awareness,

that can brighten up a shadowy day, when it seems as though I have lost my way.

Appearing as if a dove in flight, that comes to me, and gently light upon my shoulder, shining with a bit of starlight.

Whenever my eyes can see your smiling face, when I began to feel so amazed. As if my eyes can see a portrait of you,

reflecting within the sunset, such a lovely view, as it persist among the stars of night.
When I can feel the impression of your compassion, that banish the emptiness that my heart once knew.

The kind of compassion I cannot resist, realizing that when I was with you.

It was not just a lonely waste of time, or a deception of some kind of design.

Whereby with "Just a Touch of Your Love." It is all I need, to fill my mind with sheer delight, as my heart would insist.

When it seems as though I can feel the fullness of the love we once knew, that brings comfort to me throughout my sleepless nights.

Filling my heart with a warm sensation, that give me the peace of mind, that only a bit of your love can refine.

Ushering in pleasant thoughts, and vibes of appreciation, lifting my spirits up, far and wide.

As an eagle that takes to the wing, and begins to fly, into the magic that thrives high.

Whereas my memory still beholds the glitter, that once graced the beauty in your eyes, as diamonds in the sky.

As my days would be entranced in wonder and delight, bringing back forgotten memories, of moments when we were still together, seeming as though our love affair would last forever.

Whereas now, only a hint of your love still graces my heart, in which I can slightly feel, when only a small portion of it continues to be for real.

But still, it is as sweet as a taste of honey.
Perhaps taken from a period of time when our days were quite sunny.

Which takes on the connotation of two compassionate doves. That would take flight and fly into the night.

To the skies that reaches high above, where the stars would shine crystal bright.

As with the fate of magic, whereby everything always seems to turnout right.

"Just a Touch of Your Love"

THE BLOOD SUCKERS

It was a cold and bitter winter day, when the teeth of the gusting winds had just ripped through a few of the small trees, and flatted the rose brushes that grew among the weeds.

When it began slipping away, escaping out of the city of Bellverdil. A city that was spit in half economically,

existing as two distinctive parts for quite a few years. In which at such time, one side of the city's residents were living easy,

and for the other side, where certain privileges had been barred, the residents were living hard.

Therefore on the side of the city where the people were living easy, the inhabitants vigorously thrived, as nothing was to expensive for them to buy.

When on the poor side of the city, most of the residents would struggle to survive, just trying to get by.

Jobs were hard to find in Shay Town, which existed on the poorest side of the city where there was no pity.

Whereas people from the well-to-do metropolitan area of the city, known as Jones Bourrow, would hardly ever come around to Shay Town.

Then as days went by, suddenly there would be a outbreak of an epidemic, which sprung up in the city of Bellverdil. In areas where most of the wealthiest folks lived.
When some of the residents had been stricken with a severe illness known as ODS, Organism Depletion Syndrome.

Whereas for a stricken person to be absent of such illness. The patient would be in need of a blood transfusion, which was not just an illusion.

That could only be achieved by administering a certain amount of a plasma product, that would have to be extracted from a healthy donor on the up and up.

One who possessed a unique type of blood, referred to as plasma ACT, for a patient to survive, and continue to thrive.

Then as time would progress. There would emerge a man within the well-to-do part of the city's metropolitan area of Jones Bourrow.

Whose name was Joriyer Pickens, as he once held a medical position down at the state person, as a physician. Where he was mostly involved with blood work in the medical center.

Whereby some of the patients down at the prison who were once treated by him, could still recall the pains of his ill will, and the blood he had spilled.

Be that as it may, He would soon made his way to the city of Bellverdil, where he would establish an illegal, and shady institution.

That was setup on the wealthiest side of the city, to provide the stricken folks in Jones Bourrow with the much needed plasma ACT, that was necessary for a blood transfusion. Whereas a pint of such ACT plasma blood would sell for more then seven thousand dollars on the black market.

When it was well known before long, that approximately ten percent of the residents who live in Shay Town, on the poor side of the city, were the main target for the medical team.

The ones who had been endowed with the rare blood type of plasma ACT, which had been pumping within their hearts, right from the very start.

As word soon spread around, among the people on the poor side of town. That they were the ones being hunted down, like animals of prey, whether it be night or whether it be day.

Then as days faded into weeks, Joriyer would bring in other men, whom he had once trained to be his assistants.

When working as a physician down at the state prison, men who would understand the horrific formulation of his plan.

Whereby all the men that were involved in this medical practice would come together as a team. Which began when working down at the state pen.

In a department known as the Institution of Prison Reform. Such a short span of time it had been, as a matter of fact.

Whereas all these men were team players, In a scheme cooked up by the leader of the pack, Joriyer Pickens.

To exact plenty of money from some of the stricken residents who lived throughout the area of Jones Bourrow, on the wealthiest side of the city.

Then during one cold winter night, these men would all come together within the confines of their medical building.

When the moon was shining quite bright, pampering the sky with heap of radiant light. As all the men were wearing the exact, and same style of long black trench coats.

That stretched downward to the top of their black leather boots, making rules in which they would have to cope. As they flung themselves through the darkness of night, for an initiation of participation. Mapping out their plan, dividing themselves up into groups, looking to expand.

Coming up with ideas, of thoughts to be revealed. In order to get their criminal enterprise up and running, in a manner that would bring in plenty of money.

When concocting ways for taking blood from victims on the poor side of town, creating multiple illegal sales without leaving a single trail.

When they would have a toast, drinking to their new found venture, that was known as the blood game, of a system in which they had been trained.

As they were all team players, who had been highly recruited to operate from the files of their specific details.

Whereby the medical undertaking that these men carried out, when practicing down at the state pen, was one in the same.

Which was created to swindle some of the sickly people whom lived in Jones Bourrow out of their money.

Taking advantage of them when thinking it was quite funny.
When running a scam called the blood game,

Profiting of the folks who lived on the rich side of the city, mostly those belonging to the same neighborhood committee.

A primary factor to which the men had came. Men who were cunning in the medical field, taught unlawful practices that were sworn to secrecy, forever to be concealed.

However, in this particular underhanded scheme, the men who were participating in such cruel endeavor, would be dubbed "The Blood Suckers."

Whereas these men had also been trained as paramedics, who would jump behind the wheel of their automobiles.

Which had been designated as ambulances. Where at times the sirens would blast and squeal throughout the confines of the atmosphere, when the men went out to wheel and deal.

Working a con based upon their medical skills. As they would speed away whether it be day, or whether it be night, whenever they thought the time was right.

Clamoring for a big payoff without delay as their vehicles sputter along way. Whereby when playing the blood game,

the goal of these team players, was to go out and locate men and women before they could flee, no matter who the chosen victims may be.

Among the ones who had been endowed with the rare type of unique blood, which some folks referred to as plasma ACT.

Wherefore they would have to find a way to extract the blood from the chosen subjects, when working as a team.

Come up with a device to assist in executing their scheme. Wherefore this rare type of human blood was very expensive.

Then at certain times when the paramedics would go out on their runs, looking for subjects to subdue, to get their bloody jobs done.

Some of the town's potential victims would see the paramedics coming toward them. Cloaked in their long black trench coats, searching for the most vulnerable folks.

When some of the frighten people would hastily run away. Hiding in the night, staying out of sight till the break of day.

Whizzing through the streets of their neighborhoods, as fast as they could, eluding the perpetrators as it was understood.

Whereas they were anticipating that the perpetrators maybe coming after them, as potential victims. When they were cutting corners and jumping fences.

Where word would soon spread around, that the blood which was running through the victims hearts was very expensive.

That the paramedics were planning to rob them of the substance that sustained their lives, on cold and foggy nights, when the dark moon refused to shine with a bright light.

Whereby some of the potential victims would find a place to hide, till the morning sun would arise. Whether they live or whether they die.

But be that as it may, the medical assistants who were hired to extract the product were operating illegally, as well as the whole team. Buying into an unlawful scheme.

Whereas they would have to find a method in which to subdue the donors, and render them conscious.

Before they could have access to such product, and be in a position to extract the blood from the subjects as it would appear to be, as far as their eyes could see.

However in these blood extracting cases, a syringe would not always be sufficient. Since the plasma ACT was only found in a vein of ones heart.

So the perpetrators would have to use a special device with a tub attached, to retrieve the product before the extraction could ever start.

Whereby they would have to use their mouths to suck on the device. A process designed to start the plasma ACT flowing from a vein inside the victim's heart, and for this reason in part these medical assistants would become known as "The Blood Suckers."

Paramedics who were in search of someone to victimized, even if the victim would have to die.

Then as time moved on, it was a late rainy night, as the moon was dim of light. When one of "The Blood Suckers," went out into the streets on the poor side of town, as he would make his nightly rounds. In search of a blood donor.

Where he disguised himself as a transient, pretending to be a homeless man, with no place to stay, as he made his way. Deeply involved in the deadly game that they would play.

Looking for a man whose image had showed upon his computer screen, as a potential plasma ACT donor, that his eyes had not yet seen.

The subject in which the paramedic had chosen to go after was a welder, who worked alone in a welding shop, inside a small building in which he owned.

Then when the shady paramedic had found a secluded area when driving his ambulance. He would park the vehicle out of sight, as he went rumbling through the night.

When he would suddenly come upon the small welding shop, where the subject was taking a break from his work.

When working overtime, said he was catching upon some of his work that lagged behind, thought to be the hardest kind.

"Hey Mr.!" The medical assistant called out. When he would soon call out once more, "Hey Mr."

Then quickly the worker turned around. "Yeah!" The worker would yell out, answering as he turned about.

When the paramedic would ask the man if he would be kind enough, to give him change for a twenty dollar bill.

Said a woman around the corner was going to donate ten dollars of it to a special charity, which he was involved in. That she was going to give him a few dollars to spend.

However, he was playing fast and loose, not telling the truth. When suddenly he would intentionally drop the twenty dollar bill on the floor.

Right before the welder's eyes, when standing close by.
Then right away the worker would kindly stoop down to pick the money up.

When the sneaky paramedic would quickly and violently shock the worker, with his high voltage stun gun.

The worker would instantly fall to the floor, as the blood sucking man would swiftly inject the worker using a syringe.

When giving him a dose of debilitating drug inducing sedation, as he would quickly pierce the worker's heart with a sharp metal tub.

Then in haste he would began using the silver tub along with a unique device attached, referred to as the ACT pump. A name they would choose.

Where the scheming paramedic would have to place his mouth over a small opening, at one end of the device.

Whereby he would suck on it perhaps one, or maybe twice, to start the blood in the man's heart a flow. Then when the deed was done,

he would steal away into a run, keeping on the down low.
When placing the product inside a small container.

To keep it warm as he went running away, moving toward a hiding place in which he would stray.

As the worker's mangled body would lie still as he bled, when he would soon stop breathing and fall dead.

This underhanded medical practice was known as the blood game, which these men had been well trained.

And were eager to participate, whether it was the right way or the wrong way, they were bucking for a big payday.

Whereby the victims that were living on the poor side of town, the ones that were setup to betray, with their lives they would have to pay.

As the paramedics would slip through the night making their extraction rounds. Roaming about on the poor side of town.

Then as time continued to evolve. Another one of "The Blood Suckers" had entered a woman's home, where at times she lived all alone.

As the medical assistant had used his computer to research her profile, no matter when, no matter how. Something he would do whenever he went out on the prowl.

Then as he was searching about, when learning that the woman had the rare blood type as a plasma ACT donor.

He would then park his ambulance behind her house with no delays, make his way back to the woman's place. Then there! He found a way to unlock one of her doors.

When he would creep inside the place, searching low and searching high, leaving traces of shoeprints across the kitchen's floor.

As he tiptoe throughout the house in a steady stride, entering a closet when he closed the door and there he would abide.

Leaving behind shoeprint he could not hide, as his time was spent sneaking about, when he had made way inside the woman's house.

Where he would lay in wait for her, steady on the lookout. Doing his dirty deed on the down low, hoping that somehow she would soon show.

However when the woman returned, she was accompanied by her fiancé. As the couple made way, and went into the residence with grave concern.

The woman would soon notice that something was out of place, as the couple moved carefully about, noticing the shoeprints of a trace,

As the woman was led to believe that someone was inside her house, when wearing a worry look upon her face, as they were trying to sort things out.

Soon her fiancé began to search the place, with gun in hand. Going from room-to-room. Suddenly he heard a noisy when a man bailed out of a closet real soon.

Then suddenly, two shots rang out. Pow! Pow! Striking the intruder twice, as one bullet struck the man within his forehead claiming his life. As the hunt for the intruder was soon over.

When the killing of the man was swift and precise, as the blood sucker bled, near the edge of an unmade bed.

Right then and there, he would soon fall dead. The smell of gun smoke would loom throughout the house, sweeping though all the rooms.

Nonetheless, there would be no charges filed in this case, and no jury he would have to face. The shooting would be categorized as an act of self-defend, absent of suspense.

Then as days faded into weeks, when Joriyer Pickens had hired another man to be on his medical team. To replace the one who had died,

as time would slip right on by. When soon the two remaining medical assistants would unlawfully continue to extract blood from victims.

Along with the new member who had recently joined the team. When they setout, and continued to extract blood from the residents who lived in Shay Town.

On the poor side of the city, where things were not pretty, not as they seemed, as the paramedics would make their rounds.

"The Blood Suckers are coming! The Blood Suckers are coming!" Some of the folks would yell out and say, as the paramedics were running about, when making their way.

Whereby several other people had been victimized and found dead as time progressed. When all the residents in the city of Bellverdil were hoping for the best.

So in the meantime, after a few more days had unwound, another victim had been found lying in the backseat of his automobile, where he had been recently killed.

Then when the coldness of the moonlight began brushing across the darkness of night. During this particular time, perhaps a couple of days later.

Two other bodies were discover in the bedroom of the victims homes. Wherefore all the cases were found to have the same MO (motive of observation), as time dragged on.

Then during a very foggy night. The new member of the medical team had found his way out to a place that was occupied by a man known as Joell Vermard.

When the new assistant would lay in wait, hiding outside in the shadows of the man's isolated shack, that setback inside the wooded area that lies a few miles outside of the city.

As he was waiting for the man to return home, thinking that perhaps he would soon make his way back, when all alone.

Then during this particular period of the evening, when Joell was in the process of heading back toward his place,
making his way back home when traveling all alone.

His vehicle would breakdown, becoming disable before he could reach his place after leaving town.

Whereas he would setout on foot walking at a rather fast pace. As he was headed toward his isolated place, when trying to make his way back.

Foraging through the foggy night, beneath the pale moonlight. Until he would eventually reach an area near his place as he was making tracks. Carrying his belongings when hanging onto an old gunnysack.

When the new member of the medical team quietly came out of the dark shadows, as if a spook in the night, when the stars refused to shine crystal bright.

As the man, Joell, was tired and worn out from the long walk. Then quickly, the blood sucker would creep upon the man,

zap him with his high voltage stun gun that he carried around, as the man dropped to his knees, and fell to the ground.

When making a loud moaning sound, but before the cunning paramedic could pump the victim with a sedative,

that he may take his blood. The man named Joell miraculously jumped up, and began to fight with his foe, when moving kind of slow.

Suddenly the new paramedic grabbed hold of a knife that he carried around, and stabbed Joell within his side, and there the victim would soon die.

As the blood sucker would plunge the metal tub deep into a vein inside the dead man's heart, and suck out the source of the victim's rare blood.

Using a special device when taking his life. As the new paramedic would take time to clean up his mess.

After he had put the man inside his ambulance, when he drove down to a nearby muddy creek, grabbed hold of the victim's large feet.

When he would drag the man's corpse out of the vehicle,
and dump the body into the dark muddy waters.

He would once again jump behind the wheel of his automobile, and began heading back in the direction of the city, carrying a small container inside a plastic bag.

When the cops would soon roll upon him, with red light flashing. Blending in with the foggy night when they would soon approach the paramedic.

As they would began looking for a reason why his clothes were bloody and wet. Acting suspicious when the three of them first met.

They wanted to know before the man would take flight, as his ambulance was not burning its bright lights as he drove.

When the cops had pulled him over to one side of the road. When they were trying to figure things out, in regards to what the man was all about.

Wanted to ascertain the exact reason, into why he was way out there alone. When the headlights of his automobile were not even turned on.

Wandering about, deep within the foggy night. Driving a red and white emergency vehicle. Turns out that the cops soon discovered what the man was carrying inside a plastic bag.

When they immediately placed him under arrest, for the gruesome items he had, as he was carrying them around in that plastic bag.

Soon the new member of the medical team, would lead the officers back to the corpse of the man whom he had just killed, along with the blood in which he had spilled.

Where the man's body was floating in the waters amongst some of the trees that stood within the nearby creek, adjacent to an open field.

As the corpse was drifting down stream, along with patches of fallen leaves. As the window of time would reveal.

Soon the police officers would summon a special unit to have the corpse removed from the muddy waters, and transported to the coronal facility for more examinations without a doubt.

When inside the interrogation room down at the police station, the suspect would began to sing out. Singing to a tune that would make the cops jump and shout.

Confessing to the detail of the blood game and what it was all about, when he would tell all. Implicating the other men who were involved in such illegal undertaking.

Including his boss, Joriyer Pickens, as they were all to blame, for the men who had been dying, such a crying shame.

Then as weeks turned into months, all members of the illegal medical practice were arrested and brought to trial.

Charged with murder in the first degree, along with charges of mayhem. Running a deadly fraudulent scam.

Then as the trial would wind down, when it was eventually over, each of the team players who had participated in the illegal medical practice.

Were found guilty, of all the charges that were filed against them. Three of the men who engaged in the illegal operation. Were sentenced to twenty-five years behind prison walls, with the possibility of parole after serving fifteen years, based upon an appeal.

Whereby two other members who were involved within the deadly scam, including Joriyer Pickens, the man who spearheaded the illegal practice.

Were sentenced to life in prison, and when during the sentencing phase of the trial. When Joriyer learned that he would be serving life behind bars, his knees buckled.

Whereas none of these team players would be eligible for the possibility of a parole, due to the blatant lifestyle in which they chose.

"The Blood Suckers"

Bohanner And
The Killer Bees

It was a mysterious period of the year, when the ends of springtime, and the beginning of the summer season would soon intertwine.

When on a ghostly kind of night, when the moon appeared to be shining with a spooky kind of light.

At a time when the wildflowers would began twisting, and spinning as they bloomed, when springing alive quite soon.

Blossoming along with the morning sun as it began to shine sunny and bright, with a gift of morning delight.

When later that same mystic mornings, your eyes could behold what seemed to be a dark cloud of mist, as it went zipping by moving across the morning sky.

Seeming as though it was dripping with tiny bits of black oil, staining the sky with what appeared to be black gold. Moments after the curtains of dawn had drawn to a close.

Then you would realized that what your eyes were seeing, was a dark cloud of swarming bees, moving across the morning sky creating a mystic sight right before your eyes.

When at other times it would appear to be a dark cloud of smoke, as if searching for a place to hide.

When the swarming bees were making their way near a city known as Mountain Town. Flying across the countryside, where they would dropdown to take leave and hang around.

Where a young boy who was named Bohanner Crewshaw, was being raised outside the city on a large bee farm.

Where the bees would migrate, come together and mate. Live and die, take to the sky and fly. Throughout the open air of the countryside where they would ultimately abide.

When born and nurtured, for their sweet honey, and the beeswax that they would produce, when generating a business that flourished into a honeybee empire.

Where they would be fruitful when multiplying. In a place where the birds and bees could live together with ease,

and where the ducks and wild geese would take to the fresh water ponds, right after the break of dawn, till the light of day would recede.

A place where the bees were kept and cared for, raised in large groups when sharing the interior of four large separate buildings, that were called Gates.

Where thousands upon thousands of bees would live in the upper and lower sections of the Gates. Whereby each section inside of a Gate, where the bees would nestle and mate was known as a suite.

Where the bees would cling to heaps of honeycombs that exist inside the suites, within the interior of the Gates that were located on different parcel of the property.

Whereas the bee-suites were located within the interior of the large Gates. Which divided the bees into teams, as it would certainly seem.

And up from the floor of a Gate building, sunflowers and other pollen producing plants would grow. As the honeycombs inside the building were lined up in a row.

Where each Gate building included a number of suites, which were small sections created inside a Gate. Where the bees would nestle when not at work. A barn as it would relate.

Whereas the building that was located on the east side of the property was called the East Gate, and the building on the west side of the property was called the West Gate. When there were also the South Gate, and the North Gate.

People would come from miles around to buy the sweet honey, and the valuable beeswax that was created by the bees. Whether the buyers would purchase it as a tasty treat,

or buy it as a product to sell, along with the beeswax by which they could make a profit. When earning a little more money, selling the sweet tasting honey.

As time went by the boy had grown into a smart and clever young lad. Whereas he would study the existence and the behavior of the bees.

Unfortunately, there would come a time when some of the bees would began to die from the spraying of pesticide.

Which was allegedly being used to spray the surrounding crops in the open fields, that bordered the bee farm.

Where pests and other organism appeared to be causing harm, and destroying crops of the fields. Where it was assumed by using pesticide, the pests would eventually be killed.

Nevertheless, the bee farm began to suffer financial strain, when losing out on large profits which the family could no longer attain.

As the banks and other finance institutes would carryout their unlawful agenda, which had been cooked up and made hard to remember.

When they began foreclosure proceedings against the Crewshaw family. In regards to the land, the Gate Buildings, and other assets that existed within their business plan.

In relation to some of the buildings that served the operations of the business, to keep the farm up and running.

When the finance institutes would call for the loans to be paid in full, towards various financed sections of the land.

During a time when operating the bee farm had gotten hard for the family, as they no longer met the demands, due to the complicity of the finance institutes when being unfairly ran.

It would so happen as time would swiftly go by, that the parents would up and die. Due to the unbearable stress and strain that were put upon them to survive.

As they were desperately trying to find a way to get by.
When the boy's father would become ill, and his mother would constantly cry, shedding tears of sorrow till the day she died.

Then after the boy's parents were buried. Bohanner, the only son of the family, had became sore and angry, disgusted and disappointed with the banks, and other financial institutions.

Wherefore they had stripped away most of the land, that once belonged to his family for reasons he could not understand.

Then as the years had disappeared, Bohanner, the bee keeper, had entered the year of his twenty-seventh birthday. When his three sisters had moved away.

Whereas some folks would claim that something was weird about him, the way he walked and the way he talked. The cloths he would wear, when nothing could compare.

As he continued nurturing and caring for the bees, studied them and experimented with them as time would proceed.

Then due to the results of his experimentations, he would produce a chemical substance, to which he could use as a spray, turn it into a smoke like vapor.

Whereby he discovered that the product, for which he had created could be used to control the bees. Assist him in carrying out the deeds in which his mind had conceived.

Utilized the product to assure that the bees were prone to follow his commands, and do as he say, control the primitive actions that they would sometime display.

Whereby he could make the bees rise, fly high, and fly low. Command them to come, or command them to go.

He could call for all the bees to come together, or call for them to separate, whether in the afternoon or when the day was late, as you can presume.

Then before long, he would create a suit of fish-scale plate armor for himself, that he may wear the armor when in control of the bees.

That he be protected from the bees in case something goes wrong. When putting them in a trance, getting them to obey his commands, in relation to his plan as he would carryon.

Then as a source of protection for his head, and most of his face, he soon created a brass head shield with no repeal.

With two water buffalo horns that protruded from each side of the headgear, and extended into the air. Where bees could hide if ever he wanted to spring a surprise.

Then at certain times he would feed the bees a controlling chemical substance, to make them grow larger in size. Give them more resistance to the wind whenever they would fly.

When they would grow as big as a bumblebee, as far as any eyes could see. Bees with a deadly sting, whether they were stationary or whether they would take to the wing.

Then as time progressed, Bohanner would go out one late evening when the sky was still well lit, to conduct one last experiment. When donned in his suit of fish-scale armor.

Along with the headgear in which he had created, when clinging to a long wooden staff, that had been carved with the head of a cobra snake at one end of it

As he would stand on the outside near one of the Gates, that resembled a barn. Where the bees were nestling inside the bee-suites, clinging to their honeycombs when getting along.

Then as he held the staff within one hand, he would soon raise the long wooden staff into the air, when shouting out commands to the bees as with a flair.

"Hear me, oh humble bees, in a land sweet with honey. Heed to the commands of my voice," he would advise when expecting the bees to comply.

"Arise from your suites, and come out from the East Gate. Take wings and fly into the sky, just above my head within the sight of my eyes." He would say when shouting out to the busy bees, precise and right away.

Then he would grab the long curved ram's horn, that would hang from a chain which was fastened around his neck.

When into the wind he began to blow the horn, propelling the bees to come out from their hiding places as the horn would sound off. Bhooo! Bhooo! Bhooo! Bhooo!

Suddenly a huge amount of bees from the East Gate, that set on the east section of the large piece of property, would suddenly come out.

And began buzzing just above Bohanner's head, flying near and wide, as they had swarmed to the outside.

As the bee keeper was in the process of preparing the bees for an attack, as this phase of the preparation would take place.

Which was meant to assure the bee keeper, that he had full control over the bees, and that they would heed to his commands. Whenever he would put them in a trance, for carrying out the makeup of his plan.

He would then call for the bees in the North Gate to come out, then the West Gate, and the South Gate bees to come out as well, from the buildings where each team of bees were being housed.

Then when he was finished experimenting with the bees, in which he considered himself to have full control, as their obedience had been exposed.

When they would do exactly as they were told, he would then order them to retreat back to the places of their suites, inside the buildings of their Gates.

And when the procedure had ended, he would climb to the top of a tall hill, raised the cobra snake staff up into the air, when pointing it towards the sky.

Where he would promise his deceased parents, that someday he would get revenge against the financial institutes, which had deceived them.

Causing them to die before their time, when the system was operating in defiant of its obligation as their lives would become trying.

Whereby Bohanner, the bee keeper, was aiming to make the system pay for the job it had failed to do,

when inflicting heartaches and pain upon his parents, as they were aware of the trouble the parents were going through.

Whereby the financial branches had robbed them of their land, foreclosed on some of their buildings when carrying out their bogus plans.

Then as time moved along, it was early one cloudy morning, when a darkening overcast was hanging low. When Bohanner thought it was about time to go,

and make some of the financial branches pay, for the crazy and mixed up games they would so often play.

When taking unlawful advantage of his parents, as they were once full of life and so alive. When trying to hang on to the life in which they admired, till the day they died.

Then suddenly, Bohanner would get cloaked in his suit of fish-scale armor, along with the brass headgear which had the two water buffalo horns attached.

Protruding from each side of the brass headgear, as he was playing captain to the bees, when they would only heed unto his voice, which was their only choose.

Then he would make way to the building of the South Gate, where he would open the large door and setoff a smoke like vapor inside the place, casting the bees into a trance.

Whereas he would quickly go over to the rear of his black van that was awaiting nearby. Where he would then open up the two doors in back of the vehicle.

Where he had placed a row of honeycombs inside, as he was about to take the swarming bees for a ride, as his tension was raised quite high.

He would then blow the ram's horn that he carried around, when hanging from his neck. As it would sound off when he began calling out the bees. Bhooo! Bhooo! Bhoo! Bhooo!
And as the swarming bees would began making their way, he would point the cobra snake staff in the direction of the van.

Signaling the South Gate bees to fly inside the open van, when commanding them to go and light upon the row of honeycombs, as he had confidence that they would understand.

He would then quickly close the rear doors, jump behind the steering wheel, and head out to the first financial branch that had refused his request for restitution.

And when he arrived, he parked the vehicle five blocks away from the establishment. Opened the rear doors to the van, then walked to the entrance of the finance institute.

Where he would quickly blow the ram's horn for the bees to come forth. Bhooo! Bhooo! Bhooo! Bhooo! As the sound of the ram's horn would travel back to the vehicle.

When alerting the awaiting bees to come out, as they would began swarming about. When the bee keeper would pull the doors to the finance building wide open.

Then immediately, he would point the end of the staff that had the head of a cobra snake curved upon it, toward the open doors of the banking center. When the large swarm of bees would swiftly go buzzing inside the building.

Where people were running about, when most of them were desperately trying to get out. As the bees were flying over head, stinging some of the people when a few of them would fall dead.

As Bohanner, the bee keeper, would soon blow the ram's horn once more, as the bees would retreat, and make their way back to the awaiting van as they quickly fled.

Whereby a few of the people would lay dead, as the van sped away in the early part of the day, as Bohanner had made him first play.

Then soon after the police had been summoned, they would investigate the matter, as they were now on the lookout for "Bohanner and the Killer Bees."

And as time rolled along, Bohanner would take the same approach with the North Gate bees, when ready for another bee attack.

As he would blow his ram's horn that would sound off for the bees to come out from the North Gate suites. Bhooo! Bhooo!!

Whereby they would carryout the same procedure in the manner of the first attack, which would take place on a second finance building.

Then as time moved on he would use the bees from the East Gate, and then the bees from the West Gate, to carryout the same type of attacks,

against the two other financial institutions. Where lots of people were stung, and a few of them would fall dead, when the bee attacks would be exact.

Then as time progressed, Bohanner would summon all the bees, from each of the four Gates. When he made his way to a place that was called the Wall Street of the city.

Where the movers and shakers operated their business on the sidewalks of the city, perhaps a few day each week.

However during this special attack mode, Bohanner would park his van inside a back alley, approximately a mile outside the city.

When he would made way to the heart of Mountain Town, leaving the rear doors to the van opened wide, that the bees would have access to the outside.

As a large swarm of bees had followed the van, when it were also carrying the bees that nestled within the vehicle.

Where they would all come together when awaiting nearby, inside and around the van. When it was parked within the alley near their destination.

As the killer bees were covering the grasses of the ground, as if a huge dark shadow was waiting and hovering near the van, as some of them were buzzing around. Waiting in the trees when hiding within the canopy of leaves.

Listening for the sound of the ram's horn to blow, as they would take to their wings when it was time to go.

As all the killer bees inside the van were clinging to the rows of honeycombs that were placed inside the vehicle. As others were awaiting outside, squirming and hovering nearby.

When all the bees came together as a unit, within the vehicle and outside the vehicle, listening for a command. That would propel them into a moment where they would take to their wings and fly.

Then soon before long. Bohanner, the bee keeper, made his way atop one of the tallest building within the city. Where he would raise his staff up towards the sky.

When summoning all the bees as he began blowing his ram's horn. Bhooo! Bhooo! Bhooo! Bhooo!!!!

When pointing his cobra head staff in the direction of various building that exist within the Wall Street of the city.

When cloaked in his suit of fish-scale plate armor, wearing his headgear with the two buffalo horns protruding from each side of it.

Then as the ram's horn sounded, suddenly a large pack of swarming killer bees could be seen buzzing over the city,

as if a dark cloud of wavering smoke. Zipping through the streets, stinging crowds of folks as they made their way.

When people were running about, hollering and streaming that the invasion of the killer bees were upon them, as they would shout out.

When they were fussing and cursing, as some of them had been stung about their eyes and could not see, before they had a chance to flee, or getaway into the light of day.

As a large number of folks had been stung about their face and head, by the killer bees, when other lay dead.

Soon the cops would find their way out to Bohanner's bee farm, to exterminate the killer bees. Whereas the bees had been accused of causing so must harm.

As the cops setout to accomplish the task by blasting the Gate buildings that contained the bee-suites, with a bazooka.

To blow them up, and destroy all the buildings that housed the bees as they were getting ready to proceed.

Then after the police strike would be carried out, they would then arrest Bohanner, for the death of several people, and for other heinous crimes.

However when they arrived, the Gate buildings that housed the bees had been torched, and burned down to the ground.

Along with some of the surrounding trees. As smoke was rising high, reaching for the sky.

When the cops could only see, the tail end of a black cloud of bees as they had begun to flee. When moving out across the open sky, disappearing right before the officers eyes.

Whereas Bohanner, nor any of the huge amount of bees would ever again be found, as the cops would search all around, through the countryside and across town.

Wherefore the bees could not be located, not even in the branches of the trees, nor in the canopy of leaves.

Since they took to the open sky, when flying high. Leaving the past behind, as nature would turned the pages of time.

"Bohanner and the Killer Bees"